Maximos was big, fast, and his arm reached out, his hand encircling Cass's upper arm before she knew he'd moved.

His hand felt hard on her arm, his fingers tighter than they'd ever been, but she wasn't afraid. She'd felt many emotions around Maximos, felt so much sometimes she didn't know if there was anything left to her, but the one emotion she'd never felt was fear.

Love, lust, hurt, need, agony, grief, despair, hatred.

But fear? Never.

Jane Porter grew up on a diet of Mills & Boon® romances, reading late at night under the covers so her mother wouldn't see! She wrote her first book at age eight, and spent many of her high school and college years living abroad, immersing herself in other cultures and continuing to read voraciously. Now Jane has settled down in rugged Seattle, Washington, with her two sons. Jane loves to hear from her readers. You can write to her at PO Box 524, Bellevue, WA 98009, USA. Or visit her website at www.janeporter.com

Recent titles by the same author:

THE SHEIKH'S VIRGIN
THE SULTAN'S BOUGHT BRIDE*
THE GREEK'S ROYAL MISTRESS*
THE ITALIAN'S VIRGIN PRINCESS*

The Princess Brides trilogy

THE SICILIAN'S DEFIANT MISTRESS

BY
JANE PORTER

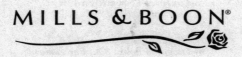
MILLS & BOON®

For Kim Young,
a fantastic editor who understands the writer and
the writing process. I love working with you! Jane

*First published in Great Britain 2005
Harlequin Mills & Boon Limited,
Eton House, 18-24 Paradise Road, Richmond, Surrey TW9 1SR*

© Jane Porter 2005

ISBN 0 263 84170 7

*Set in Times Roman 10 on 10½ pt.
01-0805-58774*

*Printed and bound in Spain
by Litografía Rosés, S.A., Barcelona*

PROLOGUE

SHE was sleeping with the enemy now.

With his gut clenched, muscles rock hard, Maximos watched Cassandra, *his* woman, *his* lover, take Emilio Sobato's hand as she stepped from the low sports car onto the sun dappled drive.

Torn between fascination and revulsion, Maximos saw Emilio's arms close around Cass's slender frame, watched as Emilio's dark head tipped, watched his enemy's mouth brush Cass's beautiful ear.

Maximos swallowed roughly, bile rising in his throat.

You shouldn't be surprised, he told himself, trying to make himself move from the palazzo window. *Women are just as treacherous as men.*

If not more so.

But Cass hadn't seemed like the type to play a man for a fool. Cass had been different.

Or had she?

His gut burned. He felt like he'd drunk a liter of battery acid.

Why had he thought she was different? How well did he know her? For that matter, how well did any man really know a woman?

The door to his study opened. He heard footsteps, and then a light hand touched his back. "Emilio's here."

It was Adriana, his baby sister, and this was the weekend of her wedding. Tonight was a reception at the palazzo honoring the bride and groom. "So I see," Maximos answered, his deep voice betraying none of his anger.

"He's brought one of his tramps with him, too," Adriana continued in the same hushed, furious tone. "How dare he do that to you? To Mama? To any of us? What kind of man is he?"

Maximos's lips curved as he stared out the window, but he wasn't looking at Emilio. He was studying Cass, taking in her chic high heels, her formfitting black lace blouse, the cut of her elegant black knit skirt which showcased the most incredible legs he'd ever seen in his life.

He knew those legs intimately.

For nearly three years he'd owned those legs, parted them, tasted them, wrapped them around his waist as he'd taken her, made her his.

And he'd made her his, many, many times over the two and a half years they were together.

She'd been the ideal lover, the perfect mistress—until she broke the agreement. And then he'd done what they'd agreed they'd do. He left. Moved on.

Now it'd seemed she'd moved on, too.

Maximos glanced at his sister, his rueful expression concealing more than it revealed. "What kind of man is he?" Maximos repeated his sister's question. "We already know the answer to that." He reached out, strummed Adriana's flushed cheek, her beautiful features tight with indignation. "A backstabber—"

"A snake," Adriana interrupted hotly.

"And a thief," he concluded evenly.

For a moment neither spoke, both lost in thought before he turned back to the window to gaze out on the palazzo's entrance where Emilio and Cass were now climbing the front steps.

Adriana stepped closer to him, pressing her face into his shoulder. "I hate him," she whispered, voice muffled. "I hate him. I'll hate him forever for what he did to you."

He reached up, cupped the back of her head. "He's not worth it, baby."

Maximos felt her tense, felt her press even closer and when her entire body shuddered he realized she was crying. "But you are," she answered, her face still buried in the crook of his arm, her voice rough, thick, the words nearly indistinguishable. "You've been Maximos, my big brother, my very own hero, for as long as I can remember."

For a split second he couldn't breathe. His chest squeezed, compressed, lungs squashed viselike while his vision went black and suddenly he was thrust back in time, back somewhere so wretched he couldn't see, think, feel. And in that moment there was no past, no future, no present—just blackness, the blackness that dwelled within the heart of man.

My big brother, my very own hero…

His sister's innocent words penetrated the darkness shrouding his mind.

Gradually the pressure on his chest eased, and his bursting lungs filled with air. He drew a breath and his vision cleared. The darkness receded and Maximos was able to laugh. "There are no heroes anymore, Adriana. Only men."

Adriana pulled away, looked up into his face, her dense black lashes damp, matted, with silent tears. "You're wrong. You're Sicilian. You're one of the great ones." Then with a kiss on his chin, she wrapped an arm around his elbow. "Come, let's go to my party. I need you there to help us celebrate."

CHAPTER ONE

"You're certain you want to do this?" Emilio asked, his tone mocking. "It's not too late to leave."

Cass stood perfectly still on the palazzo's steps, briefly blinded by the intense light of the setting sun, and refused to let herself see-think-feel beyond the moment.

She had to do this.

She didn't have a choice.

"The second you walk through the doors it'll be too late." Emilio was still talking, his words rushing over her like the warmth of the dazzling Sicilian sun. "If you're going to run scared, do it now."

Cass's head jerked up and she forced herself to look at him, focus on his face. Emilio's lips were curved and yet his eyes were hard. This was no game.

"Once inside those doors, you're committed." Emilio leaned toward her, dominating her. He'd once been Maximos's best friend and former business partner but the two were enemies now. "Don't think you can run away then."

The ugliness in his eyes repelled her. She turned her head, smoothed her black skirt, made sure her fitted lace blouse lay flat over the waistband of her narrow skirt. "I'm not running," she said huskily, before glancing up at the imposing face of the palazzo, the Giuliano family villa. The tall slender stone columns flanking the doorway supported a lovely iron balcony. Smaller iron balconies framed each of the white painted French doors overlooking the medieval piazza. It was a beautiful impressive home.

But why shouldn't it be? Maximos was a beautiful impressive man.

Beautiful, impressive and cruel.

For a moment Cass felt nothing but grief. Grief borne of loss, the pain nearly as stunning as it had been six months ago when it felt as though Maximos had driven an iron nail into her heart.

Every breath hurt.

Every thought blistered.

Every emotion, pure agony.

She drew a sharp breath, remembering, reliving the pain. He'd destroyed her. Shattered something precious inside her. In the blink of an eye. In the parting of lips. In the single beat of the heart.

Fire raced through her veins now. Fire, anger, grief.

She'd loved him. Loved him more than she thought she'd ever love anyone and it had meant nothing. She'd just been a body. In his bed.

Emilio's hand shot out, touched her arm. "If this is to work, he's got to believe we're together, that our relationship is serious."

"He'll believe it." She swallowed hard, fighting the surge of emotion. She'd never liked Emilio—not when Maximos first told her about him, and her opinion hadn't changed after a day traveling with him from Rome—but she needed him. He was her ticket into Maximos's home. "I haven't come this far to fail now."

"So when are we getting married?" Emilio persisted.

"April 16." Cass's eyes burned. Maximos despised Emilio— no, despise wasn't a strong enough word—make that hate. Maximos hated Emilio, and once Maximos saw the two of them together—she inhaled hard, sharply, pain splintering through her—he'd hate her, too.

"Where did we meet?"

"At the EFFIE Awards and we immediately hit it off."

Emilio smiled. "And how did I propose?"

"During a romantic weekend in the Seychelles. The wedding is now just six months away. Did I forget anything?"

Emilio reached out, brushed a golden-brown tendril of hair from Cass's brow. "He'll never forgive you."

For a moment she couldn't breathe, her chest burning, heart on fire.

She didn't want Maximos to hate her…didn't want him to see her as the enemy. She'd once been his. She'd belonged to him body and soul…but wasn't that why she'd agreed to do this in the first place?

Close the door on the past?

Focus squarely on the future?

Establish a future?

She put her hand to her middle, her insides churning, stomach knotting. It had been over six months, six months since the end of their relationship and she was still barely functioning, still dragging herself through the days, stunned, broken, catatonic.

Intellectually she knew this couldn't continue. She was dying at work, losing accounts, losing respect. She couldn't let a broken heart ruin her life.

It was time to move forward. She *had* to move forward, which is why she'd agreed to play the part of Emilio's adoring fiancée.

"It won't be pretty," Emilio said, his voice dropping, the warning clear and yet he was also eager. Exhilarated.

It boggled her mind how much men loved war. And this was war, a horrible war that used love and betrayal instead of bullets and guns.

Emilio had invited her to join him at Maximos's sister's wedding, suggesting they pretend to be romantically involved because he wanted blood, *Maximos's* blood, and she'd accepted Emilio's invitation because in her own way, she wanted blood, too.

Her chest burned, fire, fire, and she felt only desperation to put an end to this madness. That she could have ever loved Maximos so deeply… that she could have ever given three years of her life to him, waiting, always waiting…

"Fine," she said softly, facing the fire, letting the awful heartbreak burn, and it raged. Hot. Furious. Feverish. She'd been torn in half by love and now she'd fight, and fight hard. "I don't want it pretty. I just want peace."

She'd spent the worst six months of her life, the absolute worst months imaginable, trying to accept that she and Maximos were over. Finished. Through. And even after her body had stopped the wretched aching—experiencing a brutal physical withdrawal—her mind played games, turning every night, every dream, every man on the street into phantoms of Maximos.

She'd lived without him six months. It had felt like six years. She'd died a hundred times in the months since they said goodbye and in all that time, in all those months, there hadn't been a call. A card. A word.

He simply let her go. But why shouldn't he? She was just his mistress. He was entitled to have who he wanted, when he wanted. He was entitled to take and forget. After all he was Maximos Giuliano and she'd never asked for anything from him but sex.

Abruptly Cass moved forward, quickly climbing the villa's broad stone front steps, the sun behind them painting the door a violent red. Before she could entertain second thoughts, she rapped hard on the stately front door and stepped back.

Seconds later the immense wooden front door opened. Emilio turned to Cass, flashed her a cunning smile. "Congratulations, Cass, darling. You've done it now."

There was no time for regrets as the butler was ushering them through the vaulted entry into a grand salon off to the right, the salon's high ceiling stenciled in gold and rose and pale blue.

Emilio kept his arm loosely slung around her waist as they entered the salon even as the enormity of her decision, the incredible stupidity, hit her, a violent blow to the side of the head and she exhaled with a whoosh.

Why had she gone for the dramatic end, the death of hope, the burial of love?

Make that the burial of *her* love as he'd never loved her. He'd worshiped her body, and only then, when he'd found her convenient and available, the brutal truth made clear six months ago when she dared to ask…to whisper…for more.

Ice coated her heart and for a moment she felt like little Oliver Twist from the Dickens novel, begging, begging. *Please, sir, can I have some…more?*

And just like that Maximos had roared back, *More? Did you say more?*

Actually he hadn't shouted. He hadn't even asked her to repeat what she'd said. He'd simply given the Maximos acceptance, a half shrug, the calm, unruffled approach he took to all matters pertaining to her. To them.

Them. What a horrible little word. Them, just "the" with an *m* tacked on at the end.

Them.

But them, in terms of Maximos and Cass meant only one thing—sex. Hot, hungry, insatiable.

Just thinking of sex—Maximos—her body ached inwardly, the terrible craving still there, beneath the surface, her emotions still so volatile.

"What the hell are you doing here?"

The familiar voice sent icy prickles rippling down Cass's spine. *Maximos.*

She stiffened helplessly, the hair rising on her nape. Slowly she turned toward the voice, her body hot and then cold and hot again. From the beginning she'd been aware of Maximos as pure energy, a life force, a life force that completely overwhelmed her own. And then she saw him.

Maximos.

Dressed impeccably, elegantly, in a dark suit that fitted him as only an Italian cut suit could, he wore a sage-green shirt and tie and his golden-olive skin looked more burnished than ever, his onyx hair more polished, his hard features more beautiful. No one had eyelashes thicker, darker, longer than Maximos. No one had a mouth that smiled so rarely but kissed so beautifully.

Her belly knotted. The desire nearly as painful as the heartbreak.

She tried to look away but couldn't. She'd missed him too much. Missed his height. His build. His face. His body. She'd missed everything about him. But particularly his body. Missed the way his body stretched to cover hers, missed the way his hands wrapped around her wrists, missed the way he held her, made love to her, missed the tension of him—them—together.

There was sex, and then there was passion, and what they had was sex and passion—the hottest, most explosive, most intoxicating passion, the kind that grabbed hold of you by the throat and didn't let go. The kind that owned you, possessed you, made you its slave.

There were other big men in the room, other men with height, but no one carried himself the way Maximos did. No one with his confidence. His arrogance. His intense physical presence.

Even from across the room she felt aware of him. Too aware. And just looking at him she felt sick with longing. Missing. Desire.

Nothing in her life had ever felt as good as Maximos with her, against her.

Nothing in her life had ever felt as awful as Maximos leaving her, walking out the door.

"Good to see you, too," Emilio said, filling the awful silence.

"You've no business being here," Maximos said, ignoring Cass completely and she wasn't entirely surprised. Once he moved forward he didn't look back. He didn't harbor regrets.

"I was invited," Emilio answered, raising his wineglass in a mock salute.

"Not by my family."

Emilio allowed himself a small smile. "No, by the groom's family. My father and Antonio's father go way back."

"How extremely unfortunate."

Emilio grinned. "Are you going to call off the wedding now?"

"No. I'll just have to dispose of you. Quietly. Quickly." Maximos flashed teeth, a savage wolf snarl. "Shouldn't be difficult."

"Not with the connections you have."

"If I had the mafia connections you say I do, you wouldn't still be around." Maximos turned his head, fixed his dark gaze on Cass. "And I would have known about you," he added softly, his tone velvet with danger.

Cass's heart stopped, flipped, as Maximos's hard gaze rested on her.

She felt him consider her, felt the uncomfortable weight of his close scrutiny, and his expression, like the rest of him, was closed. Detached. Unreadable.

She'd never really known him, had she? She'd never really had him, either. And the shock of seeing him again, especially like this, was almost too great, her body awash in heat and ice, her stomach heavy, nauseous.

She'd planned this, she'd come here to confront him and yet she wondered now what she'd thought she'd really achieve.

How could there ever be peace between them? How could there ever be any resolution?

She'd loved him and he hadn't cared. The memory was like

a knife cutting inside her, slipping between her heart and breast-bone. How could she be so easy to forget? So easy to lose?

How could she have meant so little to him…?

Remnants of the old pain rushed through her, and she sucked in her breath, lifted her shoulders so that the straps of her silk bra cut into her skin. Cass stared straight forward, stared at the hard lines and angles that shaped Maximos's fierce face.

A man without tenderness. A man without softness of any kind.

Yet wasn't he—their relationship—so perfectly her? So perfectly Cass? She'd never taken the easy road, never wanted that which was simple or familiar. No shortcuts for her. Just hard work. Incredible challenges. And impossibly high standards.

"Let me show you two to the door," Maximos said now, his expression hard, blank, as he gestured toward the entry.

"Sorry to disappoint you, friend," Emilio answered, wrapping his arm around Cass and kissing her temple. "But we're going nowhere. Cass and I've traveled a long way and intend to stay."

For a moment Maximos didn't speak, his features blank, only his dark eyes betraying his anger. "This is my sister's wedding."

"Romantic, isn't it?" Emilio answered.

But Maximos wasn't paying Emilio attention. He only had eyes for Cass and his expression was hard, dangerous, so dangerous that Cass inhaled sharply and reminded herself to be brave. Fierce.

"You're really here with *him*?" Maximos asked her, his deep voice pitched even lower.

Emilio drew Cass even closer to his side. "You have a problem with that?"

"I'm not talking to you," Maximos answered, his eyes never leaving Cass's face. "I want to hear it from her."

"Why?" Cass whispered, mouth suddenly too dry, her heart hammering hard. "You walked away from me, if I remember correctly."

Maximos's lips curved and yet it wasn't a pleasant smile at all. "But Sobato, Cass? Why him?"

"Because I knew it would make you crazy." She smiled brazenly, hiding her pain, hiding the hurt wrapping her heart. She had to do this, had to get through this, had to get her old life—and confidence—back.

"Bitch."

He'd cursed her so softly, his voice filled with so much hurt and anger, that hot tears, hot hateful tears, burned the back of her eyes.

"You, bitch," he repeated roughly and this time Cass went icy and still on the inside.

She'd never heard Maximos speak to her with so much contempt in his voice and even though she'd expected it, it still cut deep, like the honed edge of a hunting knife.

She watched him turn away, his features so naked, so savage, that her heart pounded harder. Her mouth dried. She wasn't ready for this, didn't know how to do this, how to hurt the man she'd loved for so long.

This is wrong, she thought, panicked, desperate. I can't do this, and instead of tough, fierce, she felt shattered all over again, felt the awful crack inside her chest. It hurt. Her chest. Her heart burning, breaking inside. The pain was back, returning full force, a demon awake.

Maximos's head suddenly turned and his gaze met hers, his dark eyes hot, filled with rage and contempt. He was big, tall, broad through the shoulder, narrow hipped, with long strong legs. He chewed on life, tore it apart with his teeth. From the beginning she'd admired his fierceness, his tenacity, his unflinching ability to do what he wanted when he wanted. It was one of the things that drew her to him initially and it was one of the things that kept her at his side.

"You will pay," he said softly, oblivious to all but her. "Don't think you won't."

Maximos stomach churned, acid burning his gut, even as his thoughts burned black, nearly as black as the anger in his heart. To think this was the woman he'd once wanted more than any woman he'd ever known…to think this was the woman he'd trusted. *Trusted*.

And yet even feeling such anger and loathing, he still felt the impact of her lush honeyed beauty, her sensuality blatant, her curves ripe and full. Her black lace blouse molded her breasts, skimmed her narrow waist, played up her gold and amber coloring, her hair and eyes a striking topaz, glinting with fire and light. She didn't need makeup to be beautiful. She didn't need clothes or jewelry. No accessory in the world could make Cassandra Gardner more feminine or seductive than she already was.

"I'm not afraid," Cass flashed, taking a quick breath even as she clutched her wineglass more tightly.

But Maximos noticed her quick breath, her lips parted, her lips a glossy tawny lipstick a shade darker than her honey-gold complexion.

He nearly reached out to rub the lipstick off her beautiful lips, wanting to feel her skin, wanting to make her his again.

She didn't belong with Emilio Sobato. Sobato was trash while Cass was…

His.

His woman.

His.

There was no other way to think of her. No way he could ever think of her. She was his.

Only his.

"You should be," he answered, remembering everything. Like the way she looked in his bed. The way she felt beneath him. The way he could never get enough of her, how he'd reach for her two, three times a night, night after night. "I know you, Cass."

Cass took a step back, fingers damp around the stem of her wineglass. She was shaking on the inside, undone by his proximity and the intensity of her feelings.

She was still so attracted to him. Far too attracted. It was madness coming here. Stupidity. She was chasing him…*chasing*. God. She'd lost her mind completely.

She saw his gaze drop, sliding over her, a close and very intimate inspection as he examined her face, the pale skin between her breasts exposed by the cut of her blouse, the narrow fit of her black skirt as it skimmed her hips. He still liked her body.

But he didn't like her.

Cass tried to ignore the horrible emotion building inside her. You can't care, she told herself, you can't let yourself be crushed or intimidated now. You came for closure. Get your damn closure and then get out of here.

"You knew the old me," she said, chin tilting, expression bold. "But you don't know me anymore."

His dark gaze met hers, clashed, held. "And you've changed?"

"I'm not with you anymore, am I?"

Maximos smiled. *Smiled.* And she longed to knock that smug, self-satisfied expression off his face. "You would be, if you could," he murmured.

Despite Maximos's elegant shirt, the hint of sheen in the flawless fabric, the expensive dark suit, he looked more beast than man. Panther. Predator. And Cass flushed, feeling caught. Trapped. Exposed by a lie because of course he was right.

If he hadn't left her, she would still be with him. There was no way she could have ever left him. She wasn't that strong. She'd needed...wanted...him far too much.

"I hate you," she said, the words slicing her heart into shreds.

He was not beautiful, she told herself, sucking in a defensive breath, not in any way beautiful. Yet with her eyes locked with his, she could feel the heat between them. The fire hadn't died. Maybe there was no love here, but there was hunger. Fierce, carnal hunger. Touch, possession, desire.

Desire.

She swallowed, trying to suppress the curl of feeling in her belly, that electric sizzle of awareness, of knowledge. His touch had always lit a firestorm of need, his skin on hers warm, so warm, his body a pleasure and a torment.

"I'm not surprised."

She blinked, gathered her composure, willing herself to be calm, regain her cool. She couldn't lose it here, now. Not with Emilio hanging on her every word. Not with fifty-odd guests filling the palazzo's grand salon.

She turned to Emilio, touched his arm, missing the leap of flames in Maximos's dark eyes. "Should we get another drink?" She smiled up at Emilio, smiling to keep herself focused, to keep tears from welling in her eyes. She should have realized how hard this would be, should have remembered how intense the physical attraction had always been.

Hot. Dangerous.

"If you're thirsty, Sobato will be happy to get you another drink," Maximos answered. "You and I haven't quite finished yet."

She barely glanced at Maximos. "I think we have."

"And I think you forget, *carissima,* whose home you're in. You've trespassed," Maximos answered, stepping toward her. "You've invaded my home, violated my privacy. Don't think these transgressions come without a price—"

"Then name it," she interrupted, finding the courage to stand up to him, even as she ignored the shivers racing down her spine.

"What is the penalty?" she added, furious with him, furious with herself. It was all coming back, the memories rushing through her, of love and loss, memories of him, memories of the midnight trip to the hospital, memories of intense pain, and loneliness. "Tell me what it is. I'm dying to know."

"Do you two need a minute alone?" Emilio asked, suddenly helpful, deceptively innocent. "Because I could go get us drinks."

"A great idea," Maximos answered, cutting her own refusal short.

But it was all the encouragement Emilio needed, and with a casual gesture Emilio indicated he was off to find fresh drinks.

Eyes narrowed, lips thin, Maximos watched Emilio saunter off. "Your fiancé doesn't seem too inclined to protect you."

She, too, watched Emilio walk away and she hated the way her body suddenly felt weak, her legs flimsy beneath her. "Maybe because he knows you're no threat."

Maximos laughed, the sound deep, harsh, so harsh it scraped her heart, abrading her senses. "You know so little, *cara,* it scares me." For a moment he was silent, and then his head turned and he considered her. "So what *are* you doing here?"

"I already told you—"

"No. Not that bullshit. I want the truth."

"The truth?" Her voice cracked as his dark eyes settled on her, scorching her. He made her too aware of her own skin and body. They weren't touching and yet his hands might as well be all over her. Her heart thudded hard and fast. Her insides felt hot and tight. Her knees shook beneath the slim skirt.

How was it possible to still feel so strongly? To still crave so much?

Cass felt wildly out of control, empty, suspended in air. Her insides felt tender, bruised, her insides felt turned out, exposed to air.

She needed peace. More than anything she craved peace. But with Maximos there was no peace. Just anger. Just pain. Just need.

"The truth," he repeated. "Or has Sobato turned your head so completely you don't even know that anymore?"

"Emilio's been a perfect gentleman—"

"Impossible," Maximos interrupted. "But go on, tell me whatever it is you and Sobato worked out between the two of you. Give me the *truth*…if you can remember to keep your story straight."

Her mouth opened, shut. Shame swept her. Shame and indignation. Thank God there were no weapons here, nothing heavy to throw or swing, because otherwise she'd knock his smile away, knock his horrible arrogant smile off his face.

She hated him.

Hated.

How could she have ever felt any closeness, any sense of intimacy? Had the whole sexual aspect of their relationship colored her perceptions so thoroughly? Had his prowess in bed, his sexual expertise, made her believe there was more between them…or made her believe there could be more?

Now she wondered at it all, wondered at the idea they'd ever been anything but bed partners, that she'd been the way he satisfied his sexual needs.

A release, she taunted herself, and the taunting was like pouring acid on an open wound.

He suddenly reached out and touched a strand of her brown hair shot with honey-gold. "You're not really with him, are you, *bella?*"

Bella. Beautiful. He'd always called her *bella* when he touched her, made love to her and the word had buried inside her, burrowing deep into her soul.

She blinked, holding back grief and tears. Shoulders lifting, she shrugged. "But I am." She swallowed around the horrible lump filling her throat. "We're engaged."

"Engaged?" he repeated as if it were a word he'd never heard before.

Scalding tears burned the back of her eyes. "We're getting married in April."

For a moment he said nothing. His hand simply smoothed the silken strands of hair back from her face, tucking them behind her ear. "Why are you doing this, Cass?"

Her chest squeezed, lungs compressing. She didn't want to do this anymore. "Doing what?"

"Pretending—"

"It's real." She forced a smile, smiling to hide the sheen of tears in her eyes. "We're getting married. In April. In Padua."

The color drained from his face. "Padua?"

"Yes." She hoped her smile didn't look as fake as it felt and reaching up, she tugged on her earlobe, jingling her dangling gold chandelier earring. She felt sick, hideous, horrible. Just get this over with, she told herself, finish what you started so you can go home and get on with the rest of your life. "That gives us six months to plan the wedding and reception."

A small erratic pulse beat at his throat. "Why Padua?"

"Emilio said—"

"What?" Maximos was staring at her as if he'd seen a ghost, his dark eyes glazed, unseeing.

"That the city has a special significance for him."

Abruptly Maximos turned away. His features had hardened, the skin taut, pale, like polished stone. "Get out." His voice was low, raspy. "Get out before I personally throw you out."

CHAPTER TWO

"I'M NOT leaving," Cass said, jerking her elbow from his hand. "I didn't come here simply to torture you. There were things I needed to see. Things I needed to know."

Maximos's expression suddenly shifted, his dark eyes lighting, a new alertness sharpening his features. "What *things*?"

"I needed to understand why I couldn't—" Her voice broke, and the words failed her. She took a breath, wrapped her courage around her and continued. "Have more of you. Understand why you never gave me more—" And suddenly Cass knew she'd said too much. She could tell from Maximos's expression that she'd just unwittingly revealed her hand.

"You're not his fiancée," Maximos said grimly. "This is a sham, a charade—"

"*No.*" Her pulse leapt wildly. What had she done? What had she said? "It's true. I am—"

"Then why do you care so much about *us*?" He practically hissed the last word.

"Maybe because I don't want to make the same mistake twice!" She'd been through hell and back since he left her. She'd suffered more than she'd thought possible and the pain had taught her one truth: she could do anything she wanted to. "Maybe I want to understand what happened so I can damn well make sure it doesn't occur again."

His brow contorted, his expression dark, punishing. "I appreciate your thirst for knowledge, *carissima,* but this isn't the time."

"Maybe it's not convenient now, but you'll never willingly give me the time, Maximos, will you?"

A muscle pulled in his jaw. He was angry. Cass allowed her mouth to curve, one corner of her lips lifting in a small dry smile. "Maybe it is crazy to show up here with Emilio, but I wanted to see—no, I *needed* to see—what you wouldn't share with me."

"We had an agreement—"

"Sex," she interrupted bitterly, wishing she could have been content with just sex. Why couldn't sex—especially as it'd been good sex—be enough? It was for others. She'd heard that there were women who were happy with the contact, the release, and she'd thought she was one of those, thought she could do just sex if that was all Maximos could give…at first.

But with Maximos it hadn't worked that way. From the very first time they made love she wanted more, felt more, needed more. Maximos made her crave everything…emotion, passion, connection. The kind of binding connection that kept two people together…

If she could go back, do it all again, what would she do?

And Cass tried to see herself as she'd been then, young, slim, fit, hungry for something interesting to happen.

When she met Maximos she'd wanted adventure, hoped for mystery, and passion. Especially passion. It had seemed like fun, the desire for Maximos, and she'd loved the way the desire built, rising, swelling, doubling. The desire had seemed so eager and open, extravagant with potential. She'd seen no dangers, no closed doors. Just endless, wonderful possibility, and the excitement pulled her in, swept her away. Desire, have me. Hope, here I am. Love, will you come?

She'd been reckless and bold, tossing her head, inviting Maximos closer. And he'd been willing. More than willing. He'd been as eager as her. Maybe even more.

How could it go wrong?

Now she knew. Men didn't need what women needed. Men could bury their heart, even as they drove forward with their bodies. A man could empty himself into a woman and not look back. A woman held the man, cradled his body, contained his passion. She might want to forget, might want to walk away, but part of her remembered. Part of her always remembered. And the better the sex, the more exquisite the lovemaking, the more the woman wanted it to be love, and less about physical gratification.

"Just sex," she repeated numbly, trying to hide the depth of her heartbreak. Sex with Maximos had been nothing short of perfection.

His jaw flexed. His dark eyes burned down at her. "You knew the agreement."

"Things change," she answered and he didn't respond. She loved that about him. He would resort to silence whenever he didn't like the direction the conversation was heading. How nice to be a man. How admirable to be able to resort to silence, the lofty heights, the superiority of a nonanswer. But this is how it had always been between them even if she'd never let herself see it…wouldn't admit it…not until he'd walked from her life forever.

"People change," she added tautly, knowing she was goading him, and glad to have the chance to say all the things she'd never said before.

His upper lip pulled. "Don't they."

"So who is the new lover?" Cass asked, tilting her head, smiling bitterly up at him, ignoring the anger in his eyes, the cold contemptuous expression on his face. His coldness couldn't hurt her now. Cold was so much easier than fire.

"Don't be absurd."

"I've never been absurd." She handed her wineglass to a passing waiter and crossed her empty arms over her chest to hide the fact that her hands were shaking. "I've never asked you for anything. I just gave, and gave, and gave."

"You got plenty, *bella*."

"In *bed*."

"It's what you wanted."

Rage swept through her, so hot, so dry, it blistered her from head to toe. "If I'd known it'd only be sex I would have been more selfish, demanded more satisfaction. I would have demanded an orgasm every time you touched me!"

She'd shocked him.

She saw the flicker of surprise in his eyes but then he shook it off and took a step toward her. "This isn't the way to my heart."

"Good!" She leaned right into him, emotion rioting over her

face. "I don't want your heart. It's small and black and hard. In fact, you might want to see a doctor because it might not even be a heart at all!"

Maximos inhaled hard, lips pinching, nostrils flaring, his beautiful features alive with anger. "I don't have time to do this—"

"You don't have to do anything. Just ignore me. It's what you usually do, right?"

"Cassandra."

"Yes, Max?" She'd intentionally shortened his name, turning it into slang and she knew how he hated the abbreviated version. He wasn't a Max. He was Maximos. He was a ruler, a conqueror, a king.

His hand wrapped around her upper arm, fingers pinching. Her arm flooded with hot, painful sensation.

"This is my family," he said, his deep rough voice falling lower. "This is a private party, a private family function, and I won't have you upsetting my family the night before my sister's wedding."

"You're close to your family then? I had no idea. But then, we never really got to know each other that well, did we?"

"We had two years together."

"Really? That long?" She made a clucking sound of surprise. "Who would have thought?" she added, even as she laughed inwardly, bitterly. She knew exactly how long they'd been together, could remember the first night so clearly, as well as the next thousand and ninety five nights between then and now.

"So we did know each other."

"Obviously not that well," she contradicted, amazed at how steady her voice was. She'd always had a husky voice for a woman but it was even deeper, stronger than usual. Six months of crying had bruised her vocal cords, torn up her heart completely but at least she could look Maximos in the eye and not tear up. The tears were gone. He'd had something good and he hadn't cared. He'd wanted sex. He could have had all of her.

But the sorrow was in the past. The heartbreak, the indecision behind her. She'd been on a toggle board for months, struggling to get her balance, struggling to get her footing when everything just kept changing, rolling, shifting beneath her and then she finally got the picture. She didn't have to keep fighting for balance, didn't have to keep standing there struggling to hang tight.

She could just get off.

She could just get the hell off and stand on level ground again.

No more madness, no more insanity. No more love. She was leaving it behind for a new start, a new life, a life where she wouldn't lean on anyone else.

Or ask for help.

Or think she couldn't do it for herself.

She forced a mocking smile now, even as she smashed the pain down inside of her. She wouldn't be hurt by him anymore. She'd never again allow him that kind of power over her, never let him close.

"I knew who you were," she continued, "and what you did, but I never met your friends, or your family. I was never included in your real world, and it was the real world I wanted, not just the bedroom."

"And Emilio gives you the real world?"

"Oh, that and much much more."

His jaw thickened and he made a hoarse sound of disgust. "When did you start seeing him?"

Her brow creased as she pretended to try to remember. "February? March?"

His expression grew blacker. "We were still seeing each other in February. I took you to Paris for Valentine's Day."

"Then March."

"You didn't waste any time," he answered brutally, his fiercely beautiful features so hard they could have been carved from stone. He'd never seemed as Sicilian as he did now, his intimidating expression, his harsh beauty reminding her of the rocky Mediterranean island his family had called home for hundreds of years.

Waste any time? She silently repeated, thinking about what had really happened, recalling the stunning grief, and the discovery that she was pregnant. Maximos had left her abruptly in the middle of the night, left her, leaving her bed and walking out of her apartment, and three weeks later when her period didn't come she'd taken a pregnancy test. And then another. And another.

It had been so shocking, all of it, and the long, difficult months dealing with the pregnancy, and then the discovery that the baby wasn't healthy, had changed her. There had been no one to lean on, no one to go to for comfort or advice. She'd had to deal with it all on her own.

She blinked, shrugged, feigning a nonchalance she didn't feel. "You weren't coming back, and Emilio treated me well..." She let her voice drift off, letting Maximos fill in the missing pieces. "Anyway, I do hope you can be happy for us."

"Happy."

"We both do so want you to attend the wedding—"

Maximos was big, fast, and his arm reached out, his hand encircling her upper arm before she knew he'd moved.

His hand felt hard on her arm, his fingers tighter than they'd ever been, but she wasn't afraid. She'd felt many emotions around Maximos, felt so much sometimes she didn't know if there was anything left to her, but the one emotion she'd never felt was fear.

Love, lust, hurt, need, agony, grief, despair, hatred.

But fear? Never.

Maximos was huge, thickly muscled, a hundred times stronger than her but he wasn't violent, didn't need to resort to violence. Not when his touch had been so effective—enslaving. He'd owned her, controlled her just by knowing her body, knowing her response. One touch on her breast, one kiss on the side of her neck, one leg between her own and she was gone. Lost. His.

Now with his hand wrapped around her arm he was dragging her out of the room, dragging her like a madman down the narrow corridor to an even narrower, darker hall at the back.

They turned a corner, and then another and they were alone, very alone, in a very dim corridor.

Maximos pressed her against the wall, pressed his body into hers, his knee parting her legs so wide she felt splayed, exposed. "He's the wrong man for you, Cass. The absolute wrong man."

"No," she flung back even as his body covered hers. "You were the wrong man. But this time I have it right."

Maximos leaned hard against her, his chest roughly crushing her breasts, his shoulders pinning her to the wall. "He doesn't love you. He doesn't even know the meaning of the word."

"And you do?"

"A hell of a lot better, yes!"

She laughed out loud, and her laughter was like pouring gasoline on a fire. His eyes blazed, his body seething with rage. He was too angry. She'd never seen him like this. Never seen him anything close to this but she wasn't afraid, just defiant. "He warned me about you. Emilio said you'd say horrible things."

"He's playing you, Cass. Playing you just to get back at me."

"Or maybe I'm playing him, because I love being alone with him...*naked* with him."

Maximos's control shattered. His hand snaked into her hair, grabbing thick strands close to her scalp. "How is he in bed?"

"Fantastic. The most selfless, devoted lover you could ask for."

"I hear a challenge in there."

His hand wrapped tighter, twisting the long strands between his fingers. This was war. Out-and-out war. "You hear right."

"There's no way you could have with him what you had with me."

"Don't flatter yourself. As you love reminding me, what we had was just sex, and I can get great sex from many different men."

"Wrong. What we had was different."

"Not that different."

"Emilio couldn't possibly give you what you really need."

"Odd, because I've become his slave in the bedroom."

She was dousing the fire with more and more gasoline, and Maximos's anger scorched her, stunning in its strength and fury. He leaned into her, not with the shoulder bone but the muscle, and suddenly his hand covered her breast. "This was mine," he said.

"Not anymore," she retorted.

His hand slid down to cover her belly. "And this, this was mine."

"It's his now."

"He doesn't know how to touch you."

"You'd be surprised," she answered, tensing as he leisurely stroked her hip, then boldly put his hand between her legs, touching her intimately, possessively, his palm covering the apex of her thighs.

Maximos leaned closer still, his mouth near her ear. His deep voice rumbled suggestively through her. "And this was mine, most definitely all mine. Mine to do with as I pleased. However I pleased."

The heat of his hand against the warm core of her sent shock waves through her. Her legs trembled. "No."

But he didn't remove his hand. He pressed his palm up, rocking the pad of his palm against her softness, against the growing dampness, rocking against the sensitive, small ridge where every nerve ending seemed to ache. "Say what you want, but I know you, Cass, I know he could never pleasure you, the way I know how to pleasure you."

"Wrong. He pleases me *more*," she said breathlessly, aware of his body covering hers, pinning her against the wall. He was big and hard and his stubble-roughened jaw scraped her brow. "He pleases me *better*."

"You want me to make you suffer, don't you?"

She was torn between fascination and fear. This wasn't the Maximos who'd been her perfect, and very discreet, lover. He was like another man altogether, a man she'd suspected existed but hadn't seen until now. "You can try."

"Have you ever been unfaithful to him?"

The heat was growing inside her, consuming, destructive. Explosive. She felt wound tightly, too tightly. "No."

"You're getting close now."

"Then let me go."

"So you can run back into his bed?"

The idea of Emilio ever really touching her disgusted her. "Maximos." Her voice broke, and she didn't know what she wanted from him—love? Forgiveness? Mercy?

But he was in no mood for mercy and his name spoken with such desperation seemed to only push him beyond the point of reason.

He reached for the hem of her narrow skirt, grabbed at the fabric, bunching the black silk into folds to find her bare thigh beneath.

Her mouth parted in a silent gasp, desire flooding her, need and memory. And when his hand slid between her thighs to pluck aside the scrap of her thong panty, his palm pressed warm and hard against her body. Cass grabbed at him, grabbing for help, for relief, for something to explain the dark mad passion she'd fallen into.

The problem was, and always had been, that his touch made her feel. Not just physically, but emotionally. His touch made her want him, need him, love him. And as he rubbed his palm slowly across her, his fingers trailing, teasing, she shuddered. This shouldn't be happening, this wasn't supposed to be happening, yet he was right. He knew her, knew how to arouse her, control her with just a touch.

Her shudder riveted him, his gaze locked on her face, fixed on her parted lips, watching the tip of her tongue press against the edge of her teeth.

She felt helpless. And he knew it.

And he acted on it. Still watching her with that fierce possessive ownership he'd always displayed toward her, he caressed her along the seam of her, along the tender lips and then between she panted, overwhelmed by sensation.

He was teasing her, tracing her, toying with her and her legs buckled. She arched against his hand, against the maddening touch which reminded her of everything and yet gave too little.

And then he slowly slid his finger inside her, slowly drawing out the desire, building on the pleasure. More, she thought wildly, blindly, more.

But he wasn't going to be rushed, and he refused to hurry. He touched her slowly, almost lazily and her skin beaded damp, her muscles clenched in concentration. She wanted more, needed more and she pressed herself forward, pressing against his hand.

A flicker of triumph shone in Maximos's dark eyes and with a deep, deliberate stroke of his finger he showed her how she loved to be touched. Showed her that he knew her body better than she did. Showed her how much she still wanted him

But he'd never touched her in anger. Never caressed her with anything but restraint. Control. He wasn't hurting her—far from it, the feeling was shocking, intense—the raw sexual edge took her breath away, but she knew control was tenuous at best.

He stroked her deeply again, a long, knowing touch inflaming all her senses, even as her body tightened, struggling to take him, grip him, which he had no intention of letting her do.

This was torment.

This, she thought, was punishment.

Her elbows were pressed against the wall, her hands up against his chest, arms immobile between them. He'd imprisoned her so she couldn't defend herself, couldn't cover herself. Could only feel.

Remember.

Crave.

And she craved, horribly, desperately, wantonly. She knew he could do what he wanted. She'd let him take her and use her at will. Shameful, but it had always been this way between them. He was the only man who could strip away her inhibitions, who could make her be the wild child she'd always wanted to be.

From far away she heard her name being called. Emilio. Emilio was coming to look for her.

Cass struggled, felt Maximos's lips on her neck, felt the nip of teeth. "He's coming," she choked, her body convulsing as he stroked her harder, faster.

"So are you," he answered without the least bit of humor.

She shivered as his thumb flicked over her slick, sensitive skin. "Stop, Maximos. Stop, please."

"You don't want him to find you like this?"

And she closed her eyes, knowing what Emilio would see— her leg up, wrapped around Maximos's waist, Maximos's hands beneath her skirt, hands hidden between her bare, exposed thighs.

Blood roared through her head, a blush of humiliation. "Please."

"Feeling a little exposed?" Maximos's voice sounded in her ear, deep, rough, mocking. "Welcome to my world."

But he let her go. He even adjusted her thong, straightened her skirt, made sure the silky fabric hung in proper folds. "Beautiful," he said, but his sarcasm was like shards of glass scraping across her skin.

Emilio appeared around the corner. He didn't look the least bit perturbed to see the two of them together. "There you are," he said cheerfully. "You two about done?"

Maximos's lower lip curled, jaw hardening to granite. He didn't even glance at Cass. "She's all yours."

Cass clutched at the wall, legs quaking as she watched Maximos stride away, and striding he was, all massive lines of tension and fury. He looked violent. Deadly. As if he could do bodily damage to anyone and everyone.

Emilio passed Maximos with a faint mocking nod of his head and smiled as he approached Cass. "I hope I didn't interrupt anything important."

Cass didn't even see Emilio, her gaze fixed past him, vision narrowing, focusing, riveted on Maximos disappearing back.

And then Maximos turned the corner and was gone.

She trembled as she leaned against the wall, her skin still damp, her muscles strung tight, her body quivering from the onslaught of tension and sensation. Maximos had virtually destroyed her.

An annihilation of the self and senses.

"So what did the great Maximos Guiliano have to say?" Emilio asked.

She turned her head and looked at Emilio but she couldn't see him, couldn't seem to see anything but the haze of love and lust which had just consumed her.

How could Maximos still do that to her? How could he possess her so quickly, so thoroughly, strip her of control and turn her into his?

Maybe she'd always be his…

Maybe there was no hope…

"He looked upset as he walked away," Emilio continued. "Did you two have words?"

"Yes."

"How sad." Emilio's lips tugged in a sadistic smile. "Fortunately we've got three days here. By the time we leave on Sunday, Maximos won't even know what hit him."

Or her, she thought, Emilio's satisfaction puncturing her fog of misery. Emilio wanted to savor what he perceived as an early victory and all she wanted to do was slide to the floor and cover her head with her hands and cry like the little girl she'd once been.

This was wrong. Wrong every which way you looked at it. Morally, spiritually, intellectually, emotionally…

"Do you want to go back to the cocktail party or on up to our room?" Emilio asked, with a glance at his wristwatch. "Dinner will be served in about two hours."

Cass couldn't imagine returning to the salon for cocktails now. "I'd just as soon go to the room."

"I'll show you the way."

Inside the bedroom she was to share with Emilio, Cass sank numbly onto the foot of the bed.

Emilio was moving around the room, inspecting the furniture, drapes, finishes. "It's not the best room," he said, closing the door behind him. "But it could be worse."

She heard the door click shut and it filled her with fresh panic. She shouldn't be here, shouldn't be doing this. She barely knew Emilio and yet now she was supposed to share a bedroom with him for the next two nights and three days. "What's happening later?" she asked, trying not to think about the fact that they were alone together.

"The rehearsal and then dinner after. We won't attend the rehearsal but we'll join them for dinner."

"And we're really invited?"

"The invitation was sent."

"By the groom's family," she said.

"Yes."

"But this is the bride's home."

Emilio cocked his head. "Just what did Maximos say to you anyway? The two of you were gone a long time. He had to have said something. Something about you being here with me…"

"He did."

"And you told him about us? The engagement? The April wedding?"

"In Padua, yes." She sighed, briefly closed her eyes, feeling knots of tension tighten along her neck and shoulders. "And why are we getting married in Padua?"

Emilio dropped into an armchair next to the foot of the bed. "Because it's a place of particular personal significance to my dear friend Max. Tell me, what were his exact words when you told him about Padua?"

"Tell me the significance of Padua first."

"I don't want to spoil the fun." Emilio stretched, put his arms behind his neck, and chuckled. "God, I would have loved to have been there for that little announcement. Maximos probably didn't even know what hit him."

Cass stiffened, disgusted. She hated Emilio's voice, hated everything about him. Why had she agreed to come here with him? Why had she agreed to do this awful thing?

Maximos.

Maximos's betrayal. And yet wasn't she betraying him now? Wasn't she doing the very thing she objected to most?

Her conscience smote her. She couldn't bear hypocrisy and yet here she was, aligning herself with Emilio, inflicting pain on Maximos—the weekend of his sister's wedding no less.

It was horrible. She was horrible.

"Chin up," Emilio said. "The fun's just beginning."

She looked away, pressed her knuckles into the bed covering. "This is a mistake."

"He hurt you, Cass."

She shook her head, bit her lip.

"He did. He dumped you," Emilio reminded. "Trashed you. Broke your heart."

"Two wrongs don't make a right."

"Now that's the most pathetic thing I've ever heard. And you're not pathetic, Cassandra Gardner. I've heard all about you. You're ruthless at work. The original tigress. Don't change your stripes now."

He stood up, headed for the door. "I'm going back downstairs to get another drink. Are you sure you don't want to come?"

The last thing she needed was alcohol. Her head was already spinning enough. "Yes."

"Okay. But don't fall asleep. I'll want you waiting when I return."

Her head jerked up and her eyes, blazing, met his.

Emilio laughed. "Just kidding," he said, and still laughing, he exited, closing the door loudly behind him.

CHAPTER THREE

CASS stared at the door until her eyes burned, stared so long she thought she'd frozen, turned to stone.

The closing of the door reminded her of all the times Maximos had left her, all the times he'd made love to her then dressed and walked out the door without so much as a backward glance.

She'd sat on her bed more than once watching Maximos leave, feeling sick inside, feeling that she'd agreed to the impossible.

Not that she'd thought it would be impossible when she first accepted the terms of the relationship with Maximos: No commitments. No promises. No guilt trips.

But that wasn't all. There were the unsaid terms, the fine print that didn't get read the first time around. But she'd been with Maximos long enough to know the fine print by heart now.

No scenes.

No emotions.

No needs.

Nothing stated, nothing implied, nothing demanded equaled nothing denied.

It was a bitter relationship, one so one-sided that it had hurt her night and day.

She realized in the first couple of months that with Maximos there'd be no marriage, no children, no family get-togethers. No attending functions as a couple, no traveling with others.

No, their relationship was based on the idea that they saw each other when it was convenient for him, that they had what they had, that they were satisfied with what they had.

But Cass had known for over a year before she confronted Maximos that she couldn't bear to continue living with so little, or living as though she meant so little. It had quickly become unbearable being the woman on the side, the woman who was an ornament. A bit of fluff. A bit of fancy. She wasn't even his woman. She was just his mistress.

Worse, he could go weeks without seeing her. He could go weeks without needing to speak to her. She wondered if he was even aware of the passage of time. Even aware that two weeks sometimes became four weeks without a phone call. And she couldn't call. At least, she had to ration her calls.

She could call once every two months.

It was her rule, not his, but it worked. It gave her a sense of control, a way to ensure self-control. When she missed him the most she'd reach for the phone and she'd hold it against her chest. If you call now, she'd tell herself, you won't be able to call again for weeks. Months. Are you sure you want to call now? You can't sound desperate. He hates desperate. He loves the calm, strong you. He loves the gorgeous, sophisticated independent you.

Not the real you.

Not the you that is on fire with emptiness. Loneliness.

God, if he only knew the truth! If he only knew how you've changed.

Had he—this relationship—done it to her? Or had she had her own midlife crisis? You know, hitting her thirties, still single, still slim, attractive but even more alone than when she'd first started out in life.

Desperate to escape her thoughts, Cass pushed off the bed and opened her suitcase, drawing out her turquoise gown for the dinner reception that night. She hung the gown on a hanger, hooking the hanger over the bathroom door. After making sure the bathroom door was locked, she stripped and took a long soak in the tub before washing her hair.

Wrapped in her towel, she perched on the edge of the chair in the bedroom applying lotion to her arms and legs. She was nervous about tonight, worried about attending the family dinner. If she were smart, she'd just leave. She'd go now before things got even messier.

The door suddenly opened and Emilio entered the room. "Nearly naked," he said with a lecherous smile. "Nice."

She frowned at Emilio, bemused how someone like Emilio Sobato could have ever been Maximos's best friend and business partner. She knew the two had started Italia Motors together, designing and building some of the sleekest, fastest sports cars in the world before their falling-out a number of years ago. And maybe the young Emilio might have been a savvy designer, but she couldn't imagine that he hadn't also been dangerous.

"What happened between you and Maximos?" she asked, suddenly wanting to understand what had prompted this huge rift between the two. "You were once best friends."

Emilio shrugged as he began unbuttoning his shirt. "He couldn't handle my success."

"But Italia Motors was both your success."

"The engineering was all mine. Max just supplied the capital."

"Brainpower, too, I'm sure."

"He's not as smart as he thinks."

Cass studied Emilio coolly as he discarded his shirt. It sounded as if Emilio had a sizable chip on his shoulder, too. "If you're going to continue undressing, can you please go into the bathroom?"

"It's just a body."

"A body I don't want to see."

He made an exasperated sound. "We're supposed to be engaged."

He was really going to try to milk that one for as much as he could, wasn't he?

Irritably she stood, pointed to the bathroom, refusing to be drawn into another verbal skirmish. "Go, now, or I'm leaving. You choose."

He shrugged. "Whatever." But he disappeared into the bathroom and with relief she heard the shower turn on.

Cass was just stepping into her turquoise gown when a knock sounded at the door. She managed to get the zipper in the back halfway up when the knock sounded again, harder, louder.

Clutching the gaping dress to her breasts, she opened the door a crack and peeked out. Maximos. *"Ciao,"* she said awkwardly, not knowing what else to say.

"Ciao." He mocked her casual greeting.

Silence fell. She stared at him. He'd also showered and changed, dressed now in a dark suit with a stunning charcoal shirt and matching tie. He looked elegant, powerful, untouchable.

"I've come to apologize," he said stiffly.

She nodded once, her body growing hot, heat rising, flooding her face and for a moment there was just silence, but the silence wasn't quiet. She could feel his intensity, feel his tension.

There was something about him, something about his size, his stillness, his intentness that made her hopelessly aware of him, as well as herself. He made her too aware of her feelings, and her attraction.

She shouldn't be attracted. She shouldn't still feel so much and the danger was—she felt everything. Felt even more than she had before: hurt, anger, fear, need, desire. Love was gone but somehow the absence of love didn't dim the physical craving.

She wanted him.

Craved his skin, hands, mouth, body.

Needed him against her.

Taking her.

The desire whipped through her, a torment of the senses.

The sex had always been hot, explosive. Maximos's hunger had a raw edge, a primitive desire that thrilled her.

She hated him now but wanted relief.

From the memories.

From the pain.

From the impossible need.

"I'm sorry," he repeated stiffly, curtly. "That shouldn't have happened. It was wrong. Please accept my apology."

Was an apology the same thing as asking for forgiveness? No. And he knew it. Because he didn't need or want forgiveness— he was too detached, too powerful, to care what another thought, or felt.

Her eyes searched his, trying to see past the rigid shield he kept before him, but his mask was too strong, the habit of hiding himself too engrained.

"Of course," she answered just as stiffly.

His dark head inclined, the inky strands neatly combed back

from the strong planes of his face, his jaw freshly shaven smooth, and just like that she felt a strange flutter in her middle, the wings of fear and need, hope and desire and the intense emotions made her hate herself, hate him.

She wished she didn't feel so much around him.

Desperately wished she didn't still feel so much for him.

Maximos abruptly turned his head, listening to something. The shower had just turned off. Maximos glanced past her, to the closed bathroom. "He's here?" he guessed.

"In the bathroom."

"In the bathroom," he repeated tightly, disapprovingly.

"We're sharing a room."

His brow lowered, his expression dark. "Not in my house."

"Maximos—"

"*Not* in *my* house," he repeated, standing in the hallway thinking the worst sort of thoughts.

Cassandra here. Cassandra engaged to Emilio. Cassandra sleeping with Emilio.

He saw red, blood-red, and happily contemplated murder. Emilio would pay. Emilio should pay. Finally. He'd committed inexcusable crimes and he'd never even been punished.

But Cassandra wasn't intimidated and she wasn't backing down. Instead she tilted her head, met his gaze squarely. "It was the room given to me. The room given to us," she said, as if it were the most logical thing in the world for her and Sobato to be together.

"I'm changing your room," he said tersely. "Sobato will stay here."

"That's silly. I've already unpacked."

"Repack."

She gave him a disdainful look, one that said he might be Sicilian and he might be the don of this castle, but she wasn't accustomed to begging, and she wasn't going to start groveling now. "No."

And that, he thought was a most interesting answer. She'd never refused him anything before. She was a changed woman now.

"Turn around," he said, distracted by her gaping gown, which gave him a glimpse of her full breasts. He knew her body so well, knew the shape and satin texture of the breast, the even silkier texture of the aureole and nipple. "Let me get your zipper."

She shot him a mistrustful glance and reluctantly turned around.

Cass felt every muscle tighten and freeze as Maximos stepped close to her.

Closing her eyes, she held her breath as his hands settled on the zipper on the small of her back. She shivered as his fingers brushed her bare skin. Shivered again as he slowly drew the small zipper up. His hand followed the line of her spine, from the small of her back to the base of her neck.

"I think you got it," she said hoarsely as his hands lingered a moment too long at her nape.

"The dress looks beautiful on you."

Even his voice sounded deeper and the rough pitch was nothing if not sexy. The roughness strummed her nerves and desire coiled tightly in her belly. "Thank you."

"Is it new?"

"No." She turned, glanced up into his face, her gaze locking with his. "I'd had it for a while…just never had the chance to wear it before."

"Because I never took you out?"

She flushed. "Because you preferred to keep me naked in bed."

The corner of his mouth pulled but it wasn't a smile, rather a bitter acknowledgment of truth. Their relationship had been nothing if not sexual, and Cass felt the old fierce hunger fill her now. But it made no sense. How could she still want him after all that had happened between them? How could she still want him this much?

The bathroom door abruptly opened and Emilio emerged. Cass took a guilty step backward even though she knew she'd done nothing wrong but everything was getting complicated, far more complicated than she could handle.

"I thought I heard voices," Emilio said, one towel wrapped around his hips as he towel-dried his hair with another. "Is there a problem?"

"Possibly," Maximos answered tonelessly. "Depends on how you look at it."

"So what's the situation?" Emilio draped the towel across his bare shoulder.

"Cass is moving to another room."

Emilio shot her a suspicious look. "Why?"

"It's out of respect for my mother. As you aren't married yet—"

"She's not leaving me," Emilio interrupted. "We came together. We stay together."

The hard mask slipped across Maximos's features again. "Don't worry. You'll still see each other in the public rooms."

"No," Emilio stubbornly repeated. "I want her with me. She needs to be with me, too." He turned and looked at her. "Don't you, Cassandra?"

She opened her mouth to answer. "I—"

"She does," Emilio finished. "Trust me."

"I wish I could," Maximos answered regretfully, and he sounded almost sympathetic until he crossed his arms over his chest and stared Emilio down. "But that's not going to happen, is it?"

For a moment the two men engaged in a tense standoff while Cass let the word trust echo inside her head. There was that word again, trust, and it was obvious that broken trust was the fundamental issue here.

So what exactly had happened? And when?

"So what is it going to be?" Maximos prompted, arms still crossed and he looked like the Maximos of old—unflappable, immovable, the man in charge. "Does Cass get her own room, or do you both leave now?"

Emilio's expression was still belligerent. "You wouldn't throw Cass out."

Maximos nearly smiled. "Try me."

This was a new Maximos, Cass thought, one she'd never seen before. Until this weekend she'd only known the lover, not the dictator, although she'd sensed he lurked beneath the sophisticated veneer.

But then, of course, until this afternoon she'd never challenged his authority or provoked him. She'd blindly allowed him to make the decisions, trusting that he'd do what was right for her…for them.

Fool. She'd been such a fool in love.

Pained, Cass stirred. "I'll pack," she said. "I don't have much."

"I'll carry your bag," Maximos said.

"Is her room far?" Emilio asked sulkily.

"Not that far," Maximos answered as Cass quickly slipped her shoes on and gathered her remaining personal items, tucking them back inside her small suitcase. "It's close to my room," he added. "Remember where that is?"

Emilio's gray eyes narrowed. "She's my fiancée."

"So you've said." Maximos smiled, but the smile didn't quite reach his eyes. He turned toward Cass as she finished zipping her suitcase closed. "Ready?" She nodded. He reached for her case. "Then let's go."

As they walked along the upstairs hall, crossing from one wing of the palazzo to another, Maximos studied Cass's profile.

She'd changed, he thought, changes someone else might not notice but he did. It had only been six months since he last saw her but she looked different. She was still sexy, still provocatively beautiful with her amber-gold eyes and her thick tawny hair that fell past her shoulders, but her mouth was different. Harder. More brittle. And her eyes were like that, too.

"How is everything at work?" he asked, stopping before the room that would now be hers.

"Fine." But her lips compressed and she didn't sound fine.

"And at home?"

"*Fine.*"

"Cass—"

"Everything's all right, Maximos," she interrupted, her voice dropping, the pitch huskier than normal. "Let's just leave it at that, okay?"

He pushed open the door to a softly lit room, the ceiling high, arched, the dark beams stenciled in the palest shimmering gold.

Cass stepped past Maximos to enter the luxurious bedroom. White lace-edged pillows looked plump and inviting on the bed while the coverlet was a rich apricot velvet embroidered with green and gold thread. The curtains at the three enormous windows matched the apricot coverlet and fragrant pink and apricot roses filled two silver vases, one on the nightstand and the other on the antique dresser against the wall.

The beauty of it was almost unfair, she thought, watching Maximos place her suitcase on a painted trunk at the foot of the sleigh bed.

The bedroom represented beauty and romance...*love*...and wasn't it amazing how Maximos could afford to give her all kinds of material possessions, but not the one thing she craved most? "It's a lovely room," she said, aware that she had to say something, that the silence had gone too long.

"Good. Then you shouldn't mind me locking you in it."

She spun around, not at all certain if he was serious or joking. But his expression gave nothing away. His face was blank. His eyes shuttered. Suddenly she felt her lips curl up in a faintly amused smile. "As long as we weren't locked in here together."

His eyes creased. "And your fiancé? You wouldn't miss him?"

Her chin lifted. "He'd find a way to rescue me."

Maximos had the gall to laugh. "Emilio only knows how to save his own skin. I wouldn't count on him playing hero now."

"But he's already a hero." Their gazes locked, emotions hot, stakes high. "He adores me. Wants me. Unlike you."

"I wanted you."

"Naked. Compliant. Uncomplicated." It was getting harder to keep her cool, mocking smile in place. "Sounds awfully superficial, don't you think?"

"Perhaps. But I also think you're deluding yourself if you think Sobato truly loves you. Sobato cares only about himself. I've known him since primary school. I've worked with him. Socialized with him—"

"You're jealous."

"Yes." His dark eyes glittered. "I am jealous. I hate that you're together, I hate the idea of him touching you, but I'm also afraid for you." He was walking toward her, closing the distance between them. "Emilio is using you to get to me."

Maximos stared down at her from his imposing height, everything about him strong, dark, taut. He had so much power, so much sheer physical strength he made other men look puny in comparison.

"Then his plan is working," she whispered, heart thudding too hard inside her rib cage.

"And your plan? What is that?"

"I don't have a plan."

"You must. Or you wouldn't be here with him now." He took a step toward her, captured her chin, lifted her face to his. With the pad of his thumb he stroked the warm softness of her cheek gently, almost reverently. "You're going to get hurt, *carissima*."

Her heart ached. "I won't."

"You will." He looked pained, the expression in his dark eyes one of anger. Suffering. "And you've no idea what hurt is."

She couldn't look away from his dark eyes, from the sorrow he'd known, from the things he'd experienced but wouldn't share.

She didn't know Emilio, she thought. But she also didn't know Maximos. In many ways, Maximos was just as much a stranger as Emilio. Maximos had always been so private, so careful in what he said, and did.

The few details she knew about his personal life were details learned three years ago when she'd first acquired the Italia Motors account. Curious about Maximos the Great, she'd gone online one night and typed Maximos's name into various search engines to see what information she could get, but the articles and references were surprisingly limited.

As she already knew, Maximos was cofounder and President and CEO of Italia Motors. He'd been educated in Rome but still called Sicily home. And that was it.

No mention of family, one way or another. No gossip. Nothing even about Emilio other than the fact that the founding partners of Italia Motors had decided to end their partnership and go their separate ways.

"And you know what hurt is?" she asked, unable to look away from his brooding gaze.

"Yes."

The muscles in his face were so hard and tight that he reminded her of sleek polished marble unearthed from an ancient civilization.

How easy it had been to love him.

How impossible to lose him.

Looking back, she didn't have to lose him. If she'd kept silent, kept her needs buried, hidden, secret, he would have never known she wanted—needed—more. He would have never known she ached for all that she'd never had. Love. Family. Children.

But she couldn't stay quiet, couldn't continue to deny what she craved most. And in the end she'd done the unthinkable and asked for more.

Cass Gardner, taunted at work for being Invincible Gardner, had finally admitted to someone else she needed more. And admitting that she had needs, unmet needs, had been the most difficult thing she'd ever done, the most difficult thing she could imagine doing.

Maximos was proud, but he had nothing on her in that department. She was fiercely proud, too, proud of her independence, proud of her strength, proud that she had never needed anything from anyone.

But Maximos had changed that. Maximos taught her what it was to feel…what it was to dream…

Only it had been just a dream because Maximos couldn't, wouldn't, give more. Maximos had liked sex, convenient sex, and she'd watched him go even as her heart shattered.

Just remembering made her eyes sting and Cass pulled free, retreating several steps, undone by the memory of needing and losing and learning to stop feeling, stop wanting, stop dreaming.

"Let's just cut to the chase, shall we?" Maximos's voice followed her, his voice deep and bitter. "I know why you're here. Sobato knows I'm working on a new design and he's tried to get a set of plans twice now. He's brought you here to distract me, to keep me occupied so he can sneak into my office—"

"No."

"He was caught attempting to enter my office an hour ago, Cass."

"I know nothing about that."

"You were sharing a room with him. You had to know he'd left your room, gone downstairs—"

"He said he needed a drink."

Maximos's expression openly mocked her. "You have an answer for everything, don't you?"

"But it's the truth."

"The truth," he echoed softly, head tilting as he studied her.

"Tell me the truth, then. Are you really engaged? Is there going to be an April wedding?"

Everything was happening too fast. Things had gotten wildly out of control. Cass reached behind her for the edge of the bed and sat down.

"Well?" he prompted.

She promised Emilio she'd play the part for the weekend, it was just the weekend, but right now Sunday was still so far away, two and a half days away, two endless days away…

But she'd promised, promised. Cass put a hand to her stomach, nauseous, hating the charade, wanting to come clean. She'd always been honest with Maximos. Or at least as honest as he'd allowed her to be… "Of course there's a wedding," she whispered, unable to look him in the eye.

"His family isn't from Padua."

Her shoulders lifted, fell.

"Why are you marrying in Padua?"

She swallowed. "He thought it was romantic—"

"That's not why."

She looked up at him. His features were granite hard, his dark eyes fierce and fixed on her face. "Then I don't know why, Maximos. Okay?"

He was walking around her, a strange stalking that left her deeply uneasy. "It's not okay. You say you're marrying him. That means you must love him. So why don't you know him better?" He stopped in front of her, towering over her. "And why did you agree to marry in Padua? He's not from there. He doesn't have a home there and I'm quite sure you've never been there."

"It sounded romantic—"

"That's not it." Maximos suddenly crouched before her, his arms on either side of her, hands against her hips locking her in place. "You're lying, Cass. And I don't know if you're lying to yourself, or lying to me, but I won't let you do it. This isn't you, isn't like you—"

She tried to pull back but there was no escape. "You don't know me!"

"Not know you?" He laughed, his dark features twisting with disbelief. "I know *everything* about you."

CHAPTER FOUR

CASS was dangerously close to tears but she wouldn't give in to them, wouldn't give in to *him*. He'd made their lives a living hell by playing her…using her…letting her hope, dream…

"Wrong!" she choked, hands knotted, fingers fisted. "You know what you wanted to know. You believed what you wanted to believe. But one thing is truth, the other is fantasy, and I'll tell you the truth. I'm not the girl I was." She threw her head back, her face flushed, her skin so hot she thought it would peel off. "And I'm not playing nice anymore."

"Obviously not. If he can convince you to play along with his little charade—"

"It's not a charade."

"Well, *bella,* I'd be willing to bet you one hundred thousand dollars there's no wedding, and that if I called the churches in Padua, there's nothing on the books, and if I pressed you harder, you'd tell me there's no ring, no engagement, nothing of substance here." He stared into her face, his body close, too close, heat and power emanating from him in waves. "Care to make that bet?"

For a moment she couldn't answer, the air bottled in her lungs and all she could do was remember the way he'd taken her against the wall, taken advantage of her body, her senses, the way he played her then even as he did now.

Maximos did know her. He knew her too well. "No," she whispered.

"No," he echoed, a half smile shaping his lips. "I didn't think so."

He abruptly rose and she scooted back on the bed, watching

him take several steps back. His jaw jutted, his anger was palpable. "So how much is Sobato paying you?"

"He's not paying me anything!"

"So what then was your price? Because you must have been damn expensive. Did he offer cash? Stocks? Ownership in the company?"

"You make me sound like a prostitute!"

"Close enough in my mind. First you're my mistress and now you're his."

"I'm not his mistress." She jumped from the bed, marched on him. "I'm not his mistress. He's paid me nothing, offered me nothing. He knew I wanted to see you, knew I needed to see you—"

"Why?"

She was angry, so angry she could hardly see straight. Her hands clenched, her chest rose and fell. "Because I thought I still cared about you. I thought there was something between us—" she broke off, shook her head, livid "—obviously I was wrong."

"If you wanted to talk to me, you could have called me."

"You wouldn't have talked." Her eyes felt hot with tears. "You never talk on the phone. You hardly say anything even when we're together. You communicate with sex—"

"Maximos?" A young woman stood hesitantly in the doorway. Dark hair, medium height, she was very slender, almost ethereal in her pale pink slip dress, the delicate straps of the dress highlighting her perfect shoulders tanned a honey-bronze and the hint of high full breasts molded by the delicate pink fabric. "I've been sent to find you."

Maximos glanced at his watch. "I'm late," he said with a sigh.

"You are," she agreed, smiling a little, less nervous than she'd been moments ago. "And your mother is already in the car."

Maximos understood. He headed toward the door, and approaching the young woman, he kissed her on both cheeks. "My mother's fretting."

The woman's expression was mischievous. "She is your mother after all."

Cass's tummy flipped at the playful, and yet intimate, exchange. They were close, Cass realized, and it crossed her mind that they might just be more than friends…

Cass looked away as Maximos dropped a kiss on the woman's forehead. "Tell Mother I'll be right down."

"Okay," she answered, before whispering something in his ear that made him laugh and then disappearing again down the hall.

But Maximos's laugher died as he turned to face Cass. For a long moment he stared at her, his dark brows heavy, his gaze speculative. "I hope you know what you're doing, *carissima*."

His dark gaze held hers and for one second she let herself get lost in his dark eyes, in the stillness that set him apart, in the silence where he didn't share what he thought, or wanted. At least not with her. "I hope so, too," she answered.

A flicker of emotion passed through his eyes. "Be careful that Sobato doesn't hurt you," Maximos added after a moment.

"He can't." She struggled to smile. "My heart's already broken."

"Since when?"

"February." *When you left me.* But she didn't have to add the last part. He knew. She saw the realization register in his eyes and then he'd shuttered the emotion and his expression was blank again.

"I'll see you at the dinner," he said, before walking out.

And God, he was good at that, she thought, awash in pain, alive with feeling. No one was as good as Maximos at walking out.

For several minutes after Maximos left, Cass stood at the mirror in the ensuite bath and tried to finish getting ready for the party but couldn't seem to muster the energy to do her hair or apply makeup.

Hair and makeup seemed so pointless. No matter how much she dressed up the outside, she'd still feel the same on the inside. And on the inside she felt old, and tired, and very sad.

Losing Maximos in February had been awful, but the miscarriage had been the final blow, the one she couldn't seem to recover from.

And looking at her face bare of makeup she could see her age in her face, see the small creases near her eyes, the two faint grooves near her mouth. She was thirty. Single. And very much alone.

People at work called her invincible. They believed she was unemotional, unsentimental, married to her job. And maybe once upon a time she had been that tough career woman. But losing Maximos and the baby had changed all that. For the first time in twentysomething years Cass wanted something that wasn't tied to work, achievement or material success.

She wanted to feel loved. She longed to be part of something bigger than herself, something warmer and stronger.

She craved a family.

With a self-conscious gesture, Cass touched her hair, the strands still a natural amber-gold, a color close to the shade of her eyes. In the early days of her advertising career, she'd learned to play up her rich coloring by wearing black—in leather, satin, silk—or exotic animal prints like faux leopard spots and tiger stripes. She'd always worn incredibly high heels, her boots and shoes dangerous, toes pointed, aggressively sexual. She'd liked keeping people at arm's length, had enjoyed keeping others guessing.

Now looking at her bare face and loose wavy hair she knew she'd changed. Permanently changed. She'd finally understood—internalized—that success was a cold bedfellow, that achievement meant nothing if she wasn't happy, and she'd never be happy if she couldn't love and be loved in return.

Her mouth lifted in a wry, dry smile. Maybe her broken heart had actually done her some good.

Cass combed her hair, pinning it up in a sophisticated twist at the back of her head, applied her usual makeup and fastened delicate diamond drop earrings to her earlobes before slipping her feet into pale satin heels and heading downstairs.

The house was virtually empty but the butler appeared in the hall and indicated that Emilio was already outside in the car waiting.

Emilio was indeed in the car, sitting in the driver's seat, one hand resting on the steering wheel.

She saw his face as she approached, his gray eyes narrowing, his expression critical. "What's wrong?" she asked, opening the passenger door.

"I don't like it," he said flatly, fingers drumming impatiently on the steering wheel as he looked her up and down.

His petulant tone irritated her. "Don't like what?"

He gestured to her dress, and then her face and hair. "Any of it. You look…too smart, too together. It's not right. Not the image I'm looking for."

"That's too bad," she said calmly, barely able to keep her irritation from showing. This man was telling *her* about image? Image is what she did for a living, image paid her bills. But beyond the issue of expertise, no one told her how to dress, or how to behave. Not Maximos. And certainly not Emilio Sobato. "You can change if you want to. I'm certainly not. I like this dress. I like the way I look—"

"And so does Maximos." Emilio's throat worked as he swallowed hard. "I heard him compliment you. When I was in the bathroom. And it's obvious you're dressed to please him."

It was on the tip of her tongue to blurt out the truth—that Maximos knew the truth about her and Emilio's charade. She pictured Emilio's outrage and for a split second she enjoyed the idea of popping his horrible little bubble, but she knew now wasn't the time. Not before the Guiliano reception—it was Adriana's special night after all. For another, she didn't want to be alone with Emilio once he did know.

He would be angry. And outraged. And God knew what he'd do then.

"I brought this dress because I like it," she answered coolly, shrugging off his criticism, "and I'm not changing. So can we just go, please?"

But Emilio wasn't starting the car. Instead he climbed out the driver's side and walked around the sports car. "We have an agreement," he said softly, his tone almost menacing. "This weekend you're with me."

Cass didn't like his tone, or the way he attempted to intimidate her. She put her finger against his chest and firmly pushed him back. "Don't crowd me, Emilio, and don't attempt to threaten me. I know why I came here this weekend. But I don't know why you did. Do you?"

"I love weddings."

"Especially ones where you're not wanted."

He smiled. "Call me cruel, but I like to watch people suffer."

"You mean, Maximos suffer."

"Yes. I get a great deal of pleasure from watching my good friend Max Guiliano suffer." He leaned past her, reached into the car and pulled out a white shopping bag and thrust it at her.

"Now please go and change so I can continue enjoying myself this weekend."

Cass opened the tiny glossy shopping bag, pushed aside the lavender tissue paper and stared at a puddle of white. "What is this? Lingerie?"

"No. It's a dress."

"This isn't a dress." She lifted the fabric and the puddle of white became a long sheer lace and chiffon gown. "This is a slip. Something one wears under a dress, not instead of a dress."

"Whatever. The point is, I want you to wear it."

"No."

"You made a deal with me—"

"I might as well have made a deal with the devil." She shook her head, feeling the gold diamond earrings swing from her earlobes. "Because this isn't what I agreed to do. I said I'd pretend to be your fiancée, I even agreed to a phony wedding in Padua, but I'm not going to humiliate Maximos, his sister and the entire Guiliano family by showing up at Adriana's rehearsal dinner in a *slip*."

"You will." Emilio chucked her under the chin. "Because I know something you don't want Maximos to know."

"I've no secrets."

"Are you sure?" Emilio took the paper bag and shoved it at her middle and leaned close to her, very close. He dropped his voice, cocked his head and mouthed in her ear, "I know about the baby, Cass."

Cass stiffened, froze. Everything within her froze. Her eyes, her mouth, her heart, her brain…

"I know all about it," Emilio continued. "I know what you did—"

"You know nothing!"

"Temper, temper," he taunted. "But unfortunately for you, I do know. I know you terminated the pregnancy. And trust me, if Maximos discovers what you did to his child…he'll never forgive you."

She couldn't think, couldn't feel, couldn't move. It was impossible. How did he know about the baby? How could he know? And *what* did he know?

She'd told no one. No one knew. She hadn't even taken time off of work when she'd been morning sick. Hadn't even missed work the day after she'd checked out of the hospital.

"Are you blackmailing me?" she asked, voice unnaturally low. She hadn't terminated her pregnancy. It'd been a horrible miscarriage and yes, there had been procedures done afterward, but everything done had been necessary. She'd been hemorrhaging so badly...not that any of that was Emilio's business. It was nothing to do with him. It was her secret shame.

"Yes, actually, I am." He smiled. "You're going to finish this weekend, finish what we started—"

"He knows why you're here, Emilio. He knows you're interested in his new design—"

"Fine, he can't prove anything. And he'll still hate seeing us together. He'll hate it every time you touch me. He'll be sick each time you turn your adoring eyes on me, insane with jealousy every time I get a fondle, or sneak a kiss. And you better make it believable or I'll tell him everything."

Cass took her courage, her last bit of strength and wrapped it around her like a much needed cloak. She'd been hurt by Maximos, gravely hurt. Emilio could do nothing to her. "Then tell him. I'm not scared."

He chuckled. "Good girl. You keep pretending to be tough, and I'll pretend I'm a sensitive guy." His laugh faded and his face hardened. "But it's just a shame, you know, about the pregnancy, because the one thing Maximos has always wanted was to be a father. He's longed for a child." His gaze met hers and held. "Especially a daughter." Emilio hesitated. "In fact, you'd find this is quite a sensitive subject with him. Explosive, even."

There was more to this than Emilio was telling her and Cass wanted to know the facts...the truth...but she doubted she'd get the truth from Emilio. Anything he said had to be twisted. Just the way he twisted the facts about her miscarriage. "How did you find out?"

"I was at the hospital that night you checked yourself in. The woman I was dating happened to be your doctor." He looked at her, his expression speculative. "I have a copy of your medical records. It says plain as can be—D & C."

She felt the ground shift beneath her. Cass reached out, touched the car door to steady herself. "Go to hell."

"That's all it says, Cass. Nothing else. Maximos will think you ordered the D & C."

She ground her teeth together. "I didn't have a choice."

"Yes, well, you don't know Maximos very well if you think he'll find that an acceptable excuse." Emilio pushed the dress toward her again. "Now go change because there's fashionably late, and then there's just very late and I prefer to be the former, not the latter."

Back in her bedroom, Cass woodenly unzipped her turquoise designer gown, slowly stepping out of the soft fabric and laying it flat on the bed.

Even more slowly she unhooked her delicate lace bra and with trembling hands drew the sheer white gown toward her.

Even if Emilio was dating her doctor, how could he get a copy of her records? That was illegal. Patient records were confidential.

But Emilio doesn't play by the rules, does he?

No, she answered herself, and now her secret was out. She had been pregnant. And she'd suffered a horrible miscarriage—the pain had been unbelievable and even that awful pain had been nothing compared to the heartbreak. She'd wanted the baby. Wanted the baby desperately.

It didn't matter anymore, did it?

Wearily Cass pulled the slip dress over her head, down on her shoulders, smoothing the sheer fabric over her hips.

Stepping into the bathroom she looked at herself in the mirror.

It was the most indecent thing she'd ever seen. Nearly completely sheer in the front, the slip dress left nothing to the imagination. You could see everything. Her breasts, the nipples, the dark rosy aureoles. Her belly button. The shadow of her sex.

Cass drew a slow shallow breath. What was she doing? Why was she here, playing this game? It had seemed so simple in Rome when Emilio had first invited her.

She'd accompanied Emilio to Sicily to show Maximos she didn't need him anymore, or want him any longer, and then she'd return to Rome and get on with her career and her life.

Fighting a wave of icy panic, Cass plucked at the plunging

neckline of her white lace slip dress. She couldn't attend a young woman's rehearsal dinner wearing a sheer white lace dress with her breasts and thighs exposed.

Cass knew she had flaws and faults—many, many—but she couldn't do this. She couldn't humiliate another woman—much less Maximos's sister—and she couldn't humiliate herself.

But what about the baby?

Cass leaned against the counter's edge and covered her mouth, trying not to gag.

But there wasn't a baby, not anymore, and nothing Emilio could say or do would bring the baby back…

Numbly, resolutely, Cass changed out of the white lace dress and put her turquoise gown back on. She struggled to get the zipper back up before smoothing loose tendrils of hair back into the elegant twist, tucking a few new pins into the twist to secure it better.

Cass was partway down the hall when Emilio appeared at the head of the stairs.

It was hard to read his expression in the shadowy hall but his tone betrayed his fury. "You didn't change."

"It didn't fit," she said calmly, reaching for the banister but before she could start to descend the staircase Emilio grabbed her by the upper arm and dragged her back.

"I don't appreciate you wasting my time."

"Take your hands off me."

He wrapped his fingers tighter around her biceps. "Change. Now."

"I can't." But she didn't sound the least bit apologetic and she knew it. "The dress didn't fit. I'll send it home with you so you can return it in Rome."

For a moment he said nothing. He didn't move. He just studied her in the dim light of the hall.

Then swiftly he took a step toward her, reached for the front of her turquoise gown and jerked violently on the fabric, ripping the designer gown wide-open.

"Oh dear, it looks like this gown doesn't fit, either." He made a sympathetic clucking sound before turning away. "Put on the dress I gave you or I shall go straight to the reception and announce to everyone that you weren't just Maximos's mistress—but the mother of his late child."

Cass swayed on her feet, her right hand clutching the torn gown to her breast. "I didn't come here to ruin the wedding—"

"But you did want to humiliate him—"

"No." Her voice quavered. "No, I don't want to humiliate him, I'd never want to humiliate him. I love him. I've always loved him."

"You have a funny way of showing it." Emilio turned away, headed for the stairs but paused briefly on the top step. "Hurry. You've five minutes before I leave for the restaurant, and don't think I won't spill the beans. I'd like nothing better than to spoil sweet Adriana's special night with really bad news. And trust me, Cass, this would be really bad news."

Cass put the dress on and walked out of the room without even looking in the mirror. She didn't need to look in the mirror. She knew exactly what she'd see and it made her sick.

Outside, Emilio was gunning the engine. He said nothing as Cass slid into the passenger seat but in the glow of the dashboard light she saw the satisfied curl of his upper lip.

The rehearsal dinner was being held at a restaurant near the cathedral and Emilio found parking on a narrow street not far from the restaurant. Just before Emilio pocketed the car keys he reached over, tugged on Cass's French twist, pulling the pins out until her heavy honey-brown hair fell to her bare shoulders.

But he wasn't finished yet. With the tip of his finger he smudged her lipstick up over the bow of her upper lip, below her lower lip, and then with his thumb he smeared her eyeliner beneath her eyes. "Better," he said, wiping his hands off. "Nice and slutty. Just the way I like my women."

Despite her flaming cheeks, Cass steeled herself, clamping down on her emotions, refusing to let herself think or feel as she walked next to Emilio. She hated him. That's all she knew. She hated him and somehow she had to get through this evening, survive the shame of this evening until she could speak to Maximos and try to explain.

And what would she say?

She was sorry? She hadn't meant to embarrass him? She hadn't meant to ruin Adriana's wedding?

Her throat squeezed closed, and she stepped carefully over the rough curb stones in her dangerously high heels, paused in the restaurant doorway and straightened her shoulders. *Just do this. Just get through this. And then go home as soon as you return to the palazzo.*

The wedding party was already at the restaurant and Cass spotted Maximos almost immediately. He wasn't alone, either. He was standing with the young woman who'd been sent to find him earlier, the beautiful brunette in the pale pink dress, and his arm rested lightly around her waist.

Cass halted inside the door, her legs turning to lead.

Maximos was with her. She was his date.

Cass blinked, feeling thick, stupid. She didn't know why she was so shocked. Of course Maximos had a new woman. There was no reason for him not to. He was a man, a man in his prime, and he was physical. Sensual. Sexual.

Cass felt Emilio's hand in the small of her back, urging her forward but her legs wouldn't cooperate.

Of course he had a new woman, she silently repeated, but what stunned Cass, what hurt her so much, was the face that his new lover wasn't kept in the background, wasn't a woman he saw late at night or only on the weekends. This new woman wasn't a mistress…but a *partner*.

"Sophia," Emilio said, his voice in Cass's ear. "That's Sophia d'Santo. Maximos's longtime companion."

Longtime companion? Cass couldn't look away from Maximos and pretty Sophia. Had Maximos possibly been seeing another woman when he was seeing her? She suspected Emilio was lying, just as he lied about everything else and yet it didn't take much to throw Cass, not when she was already feeling so vulnerable…so ridiculously insecure.

"How long?" she asked faintly, stomach churning.

"Three years. Four. Maybe longer."

Cass glanced up, saw that Emilio was serious. But again, that could be Emilio acting. And he seemed to have a genuine talent for drama and theatrics. "You know her?"

"I knew her sister better."

"Her sister?"

"Lorna." Emilio shot Cass a sly glance. "You should ask Max about Lorna sometime. It's not often a man gets both sisters."

"*Gets?*"

"Possesses." Emilio shrugged. "But then Maximos is rich, and powerful, and connected. No wonder Sophia still throws herself at Maximos even though he treated her older sister shamefully."

Cass glanced at pretty Sophia but saw nothing in the girl's manner, or behavior, to indicate that Sophia was anything but sophisticated, and refined. "Is Lorna…the other sister…here?"

Emilio hesitated, then shook his head. "No." His hand slid from her waist and he took her elbow instead. "Let's get something to drink."

Emilio steered her through the throng toward one of the restaurant staff passing out champagne to guests. "I can't wait to see his face when he sees us," he added, dropping Cass's elbow to take two champagne flutes from one of the passing waiters. "His expression will be priceless." Emilio handed her a glass before raising his own. "To revenge."

He took a large swallow from his glass before noting her cold expression. "Come on, smile. This is fun."

She turned her head away, sickened. She couldn't do this. Couldn't pull this off. "Emilio—"

"No."

"I can't do—"

"Too late. We made a deal." His voice dropped, his hand returning to her arm. "There's no backing out now. Remember?"

She felt the lump grow in her throat. "I don't want to hurt him—"

"But I do. Badly." He reached for her chin, and leaned toward her as if to kiss her but she turned her head away and his kiss landed on her cheek. "Bad form, *cara*," he whispered.

"I never agreed to physical intimacy," she answered, forcing her lips up in a ghoulish smile as another couple passed close by, both blatantly staring at the front of her gown and Cass suddenly remembered what she was wearing.

God. What a disaster. All of it. Meeting Maximos, falling so madly in love, losing him, losing the baby, losing her mind…

Emilio dropped a kiss on the top of her head. "We're drawing attention," he whispered, nodding to the room at large. "I can pretty much guarantee that Max will be here to greet us very soon."

Cass followed Emilio's gaze and saw the way people were looking at them. Men and women alike were giving them disgusted looks and it was obvious that the elegant men and women gathered in the salon silently, strenuously objected to Emilio's presence, their objection a tangible thing. Whatever feud existed between Maximos and Emilio extended to the rest of the Guiliano family.

"And here he comes," Emilio murmured, stepping back so Maximos could get a clear view of Cassandra in her see-through gown. "He looks fit to be tied, doesn't he?" he added, twirling a long strand of Cass's hair around two fingers. "You should see his face every time I touch you."

"You're sick," she choked, trembling on the inside, unable to look away from Maximos's face. His jaw was thick, his dark eyes glittering with barely concealed rage.

Emilio smiled. "I know."

CHAPTER FIVE

CASS watched Maximos walk toward them, the air bottled in her lungs. She'd long admired the way Maximos moved, but tonight her admiration was tempered by fear. And dread. Fearful, and yet fascinated, she followed his progress through the crowded salon, watched as people parted for him.

"Cass," Maximos said quietly. "Sobato."

Cass lifted her head, and her eyes met Maximos's. He looked so angry...so disgusted. Hot tears burned the back of her eyes and her fingers curled into the palms of her hands as she prepared for the worst.

Maximos's dark gaze slowly slid over her, the examination bold, deliberate, possessive. He was letting her know—letting Emilio know—that she was his, that she belonged to him. Still.

Cass flushed beneath his intense gaze, her skin heating even as her insides contracted. She felt her breasts swell, firm, her nipples hardening, jutting against the delicate lace fabric. She felt rather than heard Maximos harsh intake, a deep swift breath that told her he'd noticed the tightening of her nipples. He couldn't ignore her, just as she couldn't help responding to him. They were a rather desperate pair, weren't they?

"You seem to be missing something," Maximos said, his deep voice pitched even lower, the sound intimate and harsh, so like him, so very Maximos Guiliano.

Cass felt herself blush again, her face and body on fire, her heart hammering wildly. Her skin tingled. She felt a hot fizz in her veins. Want. Need. Desire. "My dress," she whispered, only to feel Emilio squeeze her arm, his fingers pressing on a tender spot, but she didn't wince.

"Did you spill something on your other gown?" Maximos asked, his attention focused solely on Cass, his attention so personal that she felt as if they were the only two in the room, the only two that mattered.

How she'd missed him. Missed his arms, missed his body, missed his strength. She'd missed his endless confidence, the ease with which he spoke, moved, lived. She'd always felt empowered by Maximos. His strength had fed her own. "It ripped."

"How?"

For a moment she couldn't speak, words deserting her, thought impossible. All she saw was Maximos. All she felt was Maximos. If only she hadn't asked for more…if only she could go back, be the light and convenient mistress she'd once been. But some things couldn't be undone, and the hurt had been too deep…

Maximos reached for her, brushed Emilio's hand from her arm, and brought her toward him, brought her close enough so she could feel his warmth, smell the subtle scent of his elegant cologne. Even built as hard, as rough as Maximos was, she found him impossibly attractive. She loved his eyes, his cheekbones, his jaw, his mouth.

His mouth.

Her gaze clung to his mouth, to his incredible mouth, and his firm lips that always softened against hers…

"Your dress," Maximos repeated, his hands firm on her shoulders, his hands both comforting and a torment, a pleasure and a tease. She remembered the way his hands used to caress her, hold her, touch her. She loved his hands. Loved the way he'd made her feel. Because he'd made her feel…and feel…

"How did it rip?" he asked again.

She looked up at him, feeling blind, exposed. "Stepped on it, I think."

"You think?" Maximos's eyebrows lowered.

"It's been a long day." She tried to smile, but her lips quivered with the effort. She was fighting emotion, fighting passion, fighting memory. At that moment she thought she'd give just about anything for one more night with him. She'd give anything to be loved…wanted…cherished.

But he didn't cherish her. He liked sex. Because the sex was good. No, the sex was fantastic. But it wasn't really her that kept his attention. It was just her body.

Blinking back tears, Cass tried to lift her chin. "It's hard to keep everything straight."

"The stories, you mean?" he asked gently, but the question was perceptive. Maximos was sharp. Too sharp. She felt her smile slip and the grittiness returned to her eyes.

"It's a warm night," he added, "but not that warm." And before she knew what he was doing, Maximos was shrugging out of his black dinner jacket and draping it around her shoulders.

She bit her lip as she felt his hands clasp her shoulders, a brief touch but comforting, especially after the awful day she'd had.

"Thank you," she whispered, unable to look up and meet his eye. This was Maximos, her Maximos, the man who'd been her heart, her soul, her world for three years...

And then he was turning away, returning to Sophia where she waited for him near the front of the restaurant.

The seating for the dinner had been preassigned and Emilio and Cass had been given seats at the end of the table farthest from the members of the wedding party.

As they sat down, their end of the table fell silent and everyone turned to look at them. Despite Maximos's coat wrapped around her, Cass still felt exposed as she sat down and drew her chair closer to the table, pretending to be oblivious of the pointed stares.

No one wanted them there.

It was worse than awkward, she thought, glancing at Emilio.

"Ever feel like everyone hates you?" Emilio asked, propping his elbows on the table and leaning toward Cass.

"Yes." She felt like an intruder, and she hated forcing herself on the Guiliano family now. Weddings were special occasions, once in a lifetime celebrations to be shared with those nearest and dearest not with strangers or family enemies.

But Emilio chuckled as he whispered in Cass's ear. "Isn't it great?"

"No," she answered, lifting a shoulder, puzzled by Emilio's behavior.

Emilio didn't care that no one wanted him there. In fact, the more people excluded him, the more people whispered, the happier he became. He'd come to inflict pain and misery and he was succeeding brilliantly.

"God, I hate these people," he said abruptly, savagely. "They're a bunch of hypocritical snobs."

"And yet you came for the weekend."

"I came to make a point."

Cass took a nervous sip from her wineglass before carefully placing it back on the linen tablecloth. "And what point would that be?"

"That they can't touch me." His expression cleared and he looked almost good-humored and boyish again. "That they'll never be able to touch me. Because I'm smarter than they are. At least I'm smarter than good old Max."

She glanced down the table to look at Maximos, and just then, Maximos lifted his head, met her gaze. For a moment she and Maximos stared at each other, sizing the other up, the way they had that first night at the reception in New York.

They'd met at a business function in New York and the attraction had been immediate and intense. They'd barely made it out of the reception and into a taxi before Maximos's hand had slid beneath her dress to find her hot, feverish skin.

There'd been no looking back after that. She wanted him, and she'd wait for him, and she did.

In the beginning, the waiting had been a game. She'd see how well she could fill the time between his calls. She knew he'd eventually call—he always did—but it was her game that helped her survive.

It helped that she knew when he'd—and when he wouldn't—call. He never phoned early in the morning. He never phoned before early afternoon, and even then, it was unlikely. If he called, it would be late afternoon, from his limo, on the way to someplace, or late at night when he'd returned to his penthouse. But otherwise, he didn't call.

She wouldn't just sit there. She'd go do her own thing. But in the back of her mind, she'd know when he should call, or when he possibly might, and despite her best intentions, she'd try to be available. Which meant keeping phones on, available. Which meant being only so engaged with something that she could drop all when he did call.

It hadn't seemed so bad at first. She'd been genuinely busy that first year but it had gotten worse. Harder. It had gotten to the point that the nights between calls became a point of madness. Pain. Call me. Call me. Call me. She'd watch the clock, watch the minutes slowly change and think, I could have weeks of this…I might not hear from him for weeks still.

And that's how the anger began to build. That's when she realized becoming his mistress had been the most dangerous, self-destructive thing she could have done. Because waiting for him, waiting on him, waiting to be loved made her doubt everything about herself. Including her self-worth.

The waiting created need, and anger, and resentment. But then, when Maximos did finally call, he'd be so warm, so interested, so devoted. She'd agree to see him and being with him, alone with him, would make her throw caution to the wind. She loved making love with Maximos, loved everything about the sex and the emotion and the intimacy, and she'd lose herself, lose control.

The lovemaking was unreal in its intensity. The lovemaking made her believe in love.

And then there were the trips they took together. He'd book her into a lavish resort and he might or might not stay with her. He might or might not have business. He might or might not spend an entire night with her and the uncertainty of it all became an obsession. Why did she have so little of him? Why was their life together so brief, so short, so rigidly controlled?

As her frustration grew and her anger mounted, she knew she needed to get out of his life and back into hers. But it had been so long since she'd really thought about what she needed—other than more of Maximos—that when she looked inside herself it was just a big black hole.

"You can't take your eyes off him." Emilio's hard voice sounded in her ear.

Cass jumped guiltily. "What did you say?"

"You've been staring at him ever since we sat down." Emilio

turned her chair to face his. "He's got you in the palm of his hand again, doesn't he? One night in his house and you're his little plaything again. God, how pathetic!"

"You know nothing."

He laughed, his expression bitter, brutal. "I know women like you. Women that pretend to be smart and strong until you get them in bed. Women who act independent, but find their hot button and make them come and they're your slave for life."

She shook her head. "I'm not listening."

"Yes, you are. I can see the wheels spinning." He leaned toward her to whisper in hear ear. "So file this away for future reference. An orgasm isn't love. An orgasm is just an orgasm."

Blood surged to her cheeks and she pulled back, putting distance between them. "Thanks for the biology lesson."

"He slept with you, but he loved another."

Cass's head turned and she fixed a hard gaze on Emilio's face. "You need serious help. You know that, don't you?"

He smiled lazily. "So I've been told."

She moved her legs so they wouldn't touch his. "Is this why Maximos ended your professional association? He found out you weren't completely stable?"

Emilio's smile faded little by little. "Italia Motors was my success, not his. My car. My design, an innovative design that took the market by storm, winning us every industry award our first year alone."

"So Maximos did nothing to contribute to Italia Motors' success?"

"Nothing, compared to my contributions."

"So it wasn't his money that financed Italia Motors?"

"He wrote some checks—"

"Nearly twenty million dollars worth." She interrupted, reaching for her wineglass and giving it a little swirl. "Because the first car did win awards and yes, it did capture the public's imagination, but wasn't there a design flaw? Something in the engineering which resulted in a tragic accident and a ten million dollar lawsuit settlement."

"That wasn't my fault. Maximos was in charge of research. If he didn't run enough tests—" Emilio shrugged, hands extending "—you can't blame that one on me. I had my area of responsibility and he had his, and the bottom line is that Maximos needed me. Needed my mind, my creativity—"

"Because Italia Motors was all about your genius, right?" She leaned on her elbows. "He resented you for being the brain behind the company while he was just the moneybags."

"Yes."

She couldn't help shaking her head in disbelief. Emilio was ludicrous. Absolutely ludicrous. "Isn't this the oldest story around? Two men go into business together and one has the money and the other has the brains—"

"It's true."

"Or maybe it's true that you resented Maximos because he had money *and* brains."

"No."

"Then why are you so obsessed with him? Why should you want to make him suffer?"

"Because we had something good, very good, and he blew it. He ruined me."

Cass glanced toward Maximos. He was engrossed in conversation with the people seated directly across from him and something inside her tugged. Maximos was such a strong person, such a powerful presence that she felt him even though he sat at the far end of the banquet table.

But suddenly his head turned and Maximos's dark forbidding gaze met hers. For a long moment she just looked at him, drank him in, feeling the desire inside her stir. She missed him. God, she missed him.

Abruptly Maximos stood, crossed behind the table, walking toward Emilio and Cass.

Cass saw the taut, determined look on Maximos's face, his cheekbones jutting harshly, his jaw set. Emilio saw it, too, and smiling idly, he touched Cass's neck before running his hand through Cass's hair.

Reaching their end of the table, Maximos spoke to the man seated on Cass's right. The man stood and walked away, vacating his seat for Maximos.

Maximos pulled the now empty chair out and sat down.

"Enjoying yourself?" he asked, leaning forward, looking Emilio in the eye.

Cass felt Maximos's shoulder brush her breast and she shivered, nerves tightening.

"I am." Emilio smiled, relishing the cat and mouse game he and Maximos were playing. "Your sister is beautiful. I've never seen her look better. She's all grown up, isn't she?"

Maximos didn't even glance his sister's way. "Adriana's just twenty-one."

"A woman."

Maximos's jaw thickened. "And you like other men's women."

Emilio laughed. "Not necessarily. But I do like women." He clapped his hand on Cass's knee, and rubbed his palm in circles over her kneecap. "Especially this one."

Maximos didn't answer and Emilio's hand moved higher on Cass's leg, sliding over her knee to her thigh. "She's gorgeous, my Cass, isn't she?"

Cass couldn't bear it. She reached for Emilio's hand, lifted it from her leg. "Stop."

The look Emilio gave her was hard enough to cut glass. "Maybe it's time we went home and went to bed. You're sounding a little tired, love."

"I'm fine," she protested.

"No, you're a bitch, and I don't know what I ever saw in you." Emilio shoved his chair back and stood. "I'm going to go get a real drink. Something better than this cheap table wine."

He stalked off and Cass watched him go, insides twisted.

There was a long moment's silence and Cass stirred uneasily. She didn't know what to say, what to do, or how to make amends at this point. But she did need to make amends. This whole evening had been awful, and an embarrassment for Maximos.

"I'm sorry," she said at length, tugging on the lapels of Maximos's coat, cold despite the jacket's protection. "I've behaved badly, and your poor family, having to suffer through this show Emilio and I've put on…" Her voice faded and she swallowed. "I'm sorry. I really am."

Maximos regarded her steadily. "I was surprised to see you here with him. I didn't even know you two knew each other."

"We met in April, just after—" She broke off, surprised at a new thought. Quickly she counted back. She'd met Emilio in April at an advertising awards dinner, a dinner held three days after the miscarriage. Three days.

Maybe their meeting hadn't been by chance.

Maybe Emilio had found out about the miscarriage and intended for them to meet...

It was bizarre to think about, but made sense in an awful sort of way.

"I need to go," she said, reaching for her purse and rising. "This is—was—the stupidest thing I've ever done. I don't know what I was thinking, and you've every right to think I've gone completely mad. Maybe I have."

Maximos rose, too. "I'll take you back to the palazzo."

"No." She smiled quickly to soften her refusal. "I'll get a cab. I'll be fine."

"I can't send you back unchaperoned. I don't trust Emilio and I don't want you returning to the palazzo alone."

"Maximos—"

"I saw the bruises on your arm. He hurt you earlier, didn't he?"

Her mouth opened but no sound came out.

Maximos shook his head in disgust. "That's why I wrapped you in my coat. I didn't want anyone staring at the bruises. They were so dark. It was obvious you'd been hurt."

Hot emotion rushed through her and she had to look away for a moment to keep from crying. "I thought you were ashamed of me appearing virtually naked at your sister's dinner."

"Ashamed of your body? Impossible." He leaned toward her, kissed her temple. "But maybe it was a bit daring for my grandmother's tastes."

Cass smiled wanly. "I didn't want to wear it."

"I suspected as much." He reached into his pocket for his car keys. "Let me just let Sophia know I'm leaving. I'll be right back."

In the car Cass stared out the window as Maximos drove. She watched the neighborhoods pass by, the yellow streetlights glowed like topaz at night, the old city dark and mysterious, the narrow streets nearly deserted as the car approached the Guiliano palazzo. "How long have you been seeing Sophia d'Santo?" she finally asked, gathering her courage.

"Emilio talked about her." But it was a statement, not a question. "He said she'd been your companion for years."

Maximos didn't immediately reply but Cass felt him tense. He didn't like this subject.

"She is beautiful," Cass added quietly, her insides feeling as if they were on fire. She didn't know why she had to talk about Sophia now. Was it jealousy? Envy? Probably.

"Yes." Maximos didn't take his eyes from the road.

"And young."

His dark brows pulled. A small muscle in his jaw tightened. "I've known her nearly thirteen years."

Her chest squeezed, her heart aching. "Do you love her?"

"Cass—"

"I need to know, Maximos. I need to understand."

"Understand what?"

Her shoulders lifted, fell. "Why you didn't love me."

"Christ," he swore beneath his breath, palms pressing hard against the leather covered steering wheel. "Women. You're all impossible."

Cass folded her hands in her lap, nails dug into her skin. "Would you marry her?"

"Cass."

"Is that why you only saw me part-time? Because the rest of the time you were with her?"

Maximos pulled over to the side of the road and turned in his seat to look at her, and even in the dim light of the interior his expression was fierce, forbidding. "I was not with her. I care about Sophia, but I do not love her and would not marry her."

Cass looked at him, seeing the strong proud lines of his face in the shadowed light of the car interior. "So she's never been your lover?"

"No!" His voice thundered in the car. "No. Any more questions?"

Cass looked away. "Not at the moment."

"Good." He started the car and resumed driving. The rest of the brief trip was finished in silence. But as Maximos pulled up in front of his family's palazzo, the house having passed from one generation of Guilianos to the next for nearly five hundred years, Maximos broke the silence. "You've changed," he said tersely. "You used to be strong. Optimistic. You're so insecure now."

Insecure. That was one way of putting it. "Things were different then," she said.

"Not that different."

Cass almost laughed out loud, thinking he was joking but as she caught sight of his face, she realized he wasn't. "Things are very different, Maximos."

"Think about it. You still have your job. You have your apartment, your work, your friends—"

"But not you." How could he not get it? How could he value her love—relationships—so little? "You were everything to me."

"I never wanted to be everything. I never asked to be everything—"

"Forget it. Let's just drop it." Cass swung the car door open. They'd been sitting in the driveway, the ornate lights from the plaza shining on the deserted square, turning the cathedral façade a yellow-gold, illuminating the elegant balconies fronting the Guiliano palazzo.

Maximos pursued her up the front steps. "I cared about you, Cass. I cared more than you know, but you know you're responsible for your own happiness, just as you're in charge of your own destiny. It's the one thing we agreed on when we met, it's what attracted me to you. You were strong and independent—"

"And I still am." She took a breath. "Sort of."

"Unacceptable."

"Caring for you changed me. It made me want more—"

"But sometimes there just isn't more."

She pushed through the front door. "You say that—"

"And I mean it." He caught her by the shoulder and turned her around, the dim light of the entry hall shadowing both of their faces. "You got what I could give you. I saw you when I could. And it wasn't a lot. I know it. We were a weekend thing. Once a month, two weekends a month, just now and then."

She closed her eyes, counted to five, tried to keep from losing her temper. "Yet I was available every weekend," she said carefully, "free each evening."

"You had your own life—"

"I had work," she interrupted shortly, opening her eyes to look at him. "But outside of work you were my life."

Maximos inhaled sharply. "Your mistake. Not mine."

Heat and sensation exploded inside her. Cass shuddered at the brutal tug on her heart. How could she feel so much? How could she still hurt like this? The pain was so intense she had to smile to hold the tears back. Was this love? Was it hate? All she knew for certain was that this emotion held her in its thrall, had bewitched her mind, taken control of her senses.

What she wanted...needed...

She shook her head once, a short dazed shake, the same dazed sensation she'd had since meeting Maximos two and a half years ago. "As I said, let's drop it. Let's just call it a night. I can't fight with you anymore, I don't want to fight with you. I don't enjoy it." She felt tears sting her eyes. *Not when I like loving you so much better.*

The butler appeared, formally greeting Maximos and after turning on lights for them, quietly disappeared.

"Your coat," she said, peeling off Maximos's dinner jacket and handing it back to him. "Thank you."

He inclined his head. "I'll see you up."

"I can find my way."

"I'm heading that way myself. It's easy enough for me to walk you to your room."

"Well, in that case, since you're not going out of your way..." She was teasing him and smiling crookedly, he gestured to the marble-and-gilt staircase, where the white carerra marble had darkened to almost lavender with age.

At the top of the stairs, Maximos flicked on more lights brightening the second floor landing with its dark red paint and the profusion of oils by the Italian masters.

"This is a beautiful home."

"I don't come home as often as I should. My mother is always asking me to come visit." He sighed and then laughed. "Seems

I can't make anybody happy. You never saw enough of me. My family doesn't see enough of me—"

She shot him a swift glance, sizing him up, seeing all at once his magnificent profile, the dark thick fringe of eyelash, the sultry coloring contradicted by such fierce, masculine features. He was gorgeous. Glorious. Proud. Sicilian. And obviously not interested in a long-term, monogamous relationship. "Then who does?"

"Good question," he answered, walking her to her room, again turning on lights for her, before crossing to the windows and drawing the heavy velvet curtains closed. "I suppose my staff sees quite a bit of me. Clients. Customers. Automotive engineers."

"You're introducing a new car in the new year?"

"It's being unveiled soon."

"Exciting."

"Mmmm," he said, noncommittal, before changing subjects. "The house is old, but it does have an intercom. My mother insisted on it when my father was ill several years ago. You can call the kitchen if you need anything to eat or drink, or if you require something from housekeeping."

"Thank you," she said, thinking that just looking at him made her hurt. Just looking into his dark eyes made her want.

He'd discovered her turquoise gown on the bed. "What the hell happened to your dress?"

When she didn't answer she saw him lift her ruined gown, the delicate fabric of the bodice in shreds. Maximos's brow furrowed, his expression darkening. "Sobato did this."

She didn't have to say anything. Maximos knew, and he swore softly. "I should just kill him and be done with all of this."

She took the gown from him, balling it up and tossing it into a chair in the corner. "Don't say that."

"Why not?" His tone turned savage. "He's made my life a living hell for far too long."

"I'm sorry," she said, wanting to go to him, touch him but she didn't dare. He was too angry and she was too unsure of herself. Once she knew how to please him but that seemed like light-years ago. "I shouldn't have come here with him, shouldn't have done this, shouldn't have needed what I needed."

"And that was?"

"Closure."

"Right." His voice was quiet, thoughtful. "Closure." He looked at her. "Is that possible? Having seen me, do you think you'll have that…closure?"

No. Never. Because she'd never forget him, never stop loving him. It was impossible. He might as well be part of her. "I hope so."

CHAPTER SIX

"THAT's good," he said, smiling thinly but the smile didn't reach his eyes. "And at least Sobato's gone. You don't have to worry about him anymore. His things have been removed from his room. He won't be back."

Emilio was gone? Cass felt a wave of relief. "What do you mean?"

"He won't be returning to the palazzo, or attending the wedding. I made sure of that before we left the restaurant tonight."

She felt weak, her legs wobbly, and she didn't even know why. "You can do that?"

"My security detail can."

She moved to the window, touched one velvet panel, the velvet soft, warm, pliable beneath her fingertips. "I didn't know you had security."

"I don't when I travel. But here at home when the family gathers at the palazzo, or when we host a party, particularly one like my sister's wedding where we have many high profile guests attending, it's wise to take precautions."

"That's how you knew Emilio was trying to break into your office?"

"We caught him on one of the security cameras."

She glanced up, checked the ceiling and corners of the room for possible cameras. "You don't have any in the bedrooms, do you?"

Maximos smiled faintly. "I believe that's considered an invasion of privacy."

"Good." A little of her tension eased. "We agree on something at least."

Maximos stepped toward her, adjusted the strap on her white slip dress, smoothing the fabric on her bare golden shoulder. The touch of his fingers on her skin made her shiver, body and nerves tingling. "We probably still agree on quite a bit."

She shivered again as his fingertip traced the low neckline and the lace panel covering her breast. "Careful," she murmured, voice low and husky.

His hand fell away. "Are you dating anyone?"

Was she dating anyone? What kind of question was that? Hadn't he been listening to a single thing she'd said today? "I'm not dating."

"Why not?"

Did he really mean to hurt her, or was he honestly so oblivious to the depth of her feelings? It took her a moment to manage a careless shrug. "I do get asked out." Not that she ever said yes, but he didn't have to know that. Since he clearly didn't care.

"And do you go out?" he persisted.

"I haven't been in the mood." First there was the heartbreak, then the discovery of the pregnancy and then the miscarriage. Not exactly the right mind frame for meeting—or dating—new men.

"You're too young not to go out, find real happiness."

"Because with you it wasn't real happiness?"

"I was never an option."

She gritted her teeth, not understanding, not ever understanding why it was that he'd ruled himself out as a possibility, why he'd have her body but not her heart. "I hate it when you do that."

"Do what?"

"Make decisions for me. Decide what it is I can or can't have, what it is I need or don't need." The anger was building. Hot, terrible and fierce. "You might know what you need, Maximos, and you might know what you want. But you don't know the first thing about me." The emotion felt hot and strangled inside. "You never even tried."

Silence stretched, a long uncomfortable silence that made the hair on her nape rise.

"And yet you let it continue for two years," Maximos said finally, his voice a soft drawl.

She gritted her teeth, stifling the pain. "Stupid, isn't it? If I were smart, I would have bailed early on."

"If I were smart I would have moved on six months ago."

Her heart did a painful lurch. "You haven't moved on?"

The corner of his mouth lifted in a faint, mocking smile. "You're surprisingly difficult to forget."

"Maximos." His name came out strangled, her voice strangled, everything inside her tightening up. What did he mean by that? And why had she ever loved *him*? Why him? There were so many men in the world, so many men who had been interested in her, fiercely devoted, but she'd never cared about any of them, never cared one way or the other until Maximos.

He now reached for her, his hand cupping the back of her head, his fingers curving, briefly tangling in her long hair before falling away. "So difficult, I find myself not wanting any other woman yet."

"Yet?"

He ignored her comment. "And you should know that I never slept with any other woman while I was sleeping with you."

Sleeping. Slept.

Her throat squeezed, constricting nearly as tight as her heart. It crossed her mind that she should stop talking now, that even though she had questions she probably wouldn't want answers.

But she'd come too far. Waited too long. Common sense was a thing of the past. "So I was your only sexual partner?"

"Yes."

"For the entire two years?"

She felt rather than saw him step closer, felt the sudden sizzle of energy, the electric sexual tension that always hummed between them. "Yes."

Yes. Her heart did a double thump, hard, uneven, fast. Too fast. He was now standing too close. "And there's been no one since?"

"Cass—"

"I have to know."

"Why? What good will it do? If I had a one-night stand with some nameless woman, will it change anything between us?"

"Maybe. Possibly." She gave him her most evil eye. "No."

"So?"

"But did you?"

He made a hoarse sound, part exasperation, part amusement. *"No."*

She breathed in, breathing in the achingly familiar scent of him, feeling his warmth, his sheer physical strength. Even without him touching her she could remember the caress of his hand, the heat of his palm, the way his fingers wrapped around hers.

With him she'd known a life no one else had ever shown her. Known emotion, passion, a scope of feeling that had been everything she'd ever wanted—and more and the desire returned full force.

Her belly clenched. Her legs felt odd, and she kept crossing her legs, holding the emptiness in, fighting the ache as if desire could be so easily answered.

She wanted him.

She needed him to drag her to him, make her straddle his lap, sinking deeply into him.

She remembered it all, remembered the way he'd bury himself in her, remembered the way she'd wrap herself around him. Remembered how slowly he'd take her, love her, remembered how he'd drag the pleasure out.

She wanted him now. She wanted release. A reprieve.

But it wasn't going to happen. It couldn't. Not with things so complicated between them now. "You should go back to the restaurant," she said, trying to be practical, do the right thing. "Sophia's waiting—"

"She's not. She's going home with her parents. Her family lives not far from here. Besides, as I told you, we're not together, not the way you think."

"But Emilio said—"

"And you believed him?"

She licked her bottom lip carefully. "I wasn't sure what to believe."

Maximos looked at her, no emotion anywhere in his dark eyes, on his face, and again the silence stretched, the tension growing. "You should have never come here."

Cass swallowed the knot of desire burning in her throat, matching the fire in her lower belly. She ached all over, hot with want, hot with need. "You're probably right."

"Maybe you're the one that should leave," he added. "Maybe you should run."

Run, she repeated silently, thinking it was the same word Emilio had used earlier on the palazzo's front steps. *Run.*

Run to whom? There was no one to go to.

Run where? Back to Rome where she still lived and worked? Back to the luxurious, sprawling penthouse suite Maximos had bought for her three years ago when he'd wanted her more than life itself? When he'd been determined to have her—no matter the cost?

"Yes," she agreed, knowing intellectually that she had to leave this place and never come back, never speak to Maximos again, never have contact with him because she'd never get over him, never recover from him, if she thought, hoped, believed she might still have a chance.

"This isn't what we should be doing." His voice was quiet, but she sensed the storm beneath the calm. "We shouldn't be alone, not like this."

"I know. I'm a wicked woman, and bad for your reputation."

He grimaced. "That's the problem. I like wicked women. And I don't trust myself alone with you."

It was what she wanted, what she needed to hear, and it should have made her feel victorious but it only made her afraid. If he made love to her now, he'd blame her. If he lost control, it would be because of lust, not love. And she wanted love, *his* love. She'd had his body but God help her, this time she wanted his heart.

"Then you better go now." Her voice cracked. "Because I won't be the bad girl anymore. I'm actually not that bad."

"You want me to go?"

Yes. No.

No.

No.

Acid tears filled her eyes and she drew a breath that cut her from the inside out. "Yes."

"Yes?"

He'd done this to her, she thought, struggling to nod even as she stared up into his hard beautiful face, losing herself in his dark silent eyes. He'd brought her to this. He knew her better than anyone—had made love to her—and still he'd cast her off.

She had to get over him, had to get rid of him. If she were smart she'd take his heart out.

But first she'd have to rip out her own.

The bitterest of emotions filled her and she looked away, precariously close to losing control.

Either he needed to go or she did, but this couldn't continue, not a minute longer. She missed him—Maximos—the man she loved and that was the man she wanted, not this hard distant stranger.

Silence filled the room, and then the sound of footsteps, Maximos's footsteps and then came the firm but distinct closing of the bedroom door.

Cass jerked around, turning swiftly toward the door, tears flooding her eyes.

But Maximos wasn't gone. He was there, at the door, and he was turning the antiquated dead bolt, locking them in.

"What now?" he asked, watching her.

She shook her head, nervous. Overwhelmed. Even scared. She was defenseless when it came to Maximos and she bit her lip, biting so hard she tasted blood. *Don't get emotional,* she told herself, *don't fall apart now.* "You're not making this easy," she said.

His laugh was low, mocking. "You were the one that came to me."

"I didn't have a choice."

"No?"

"No." Her lips trembled and she struggled to smile. "I don't think I've had a choice since I met you. I knew…knew from the first time I saw you." Her shoulders lifted, a slight shiver of cold and nerves. "I've always known when something big happens, I know it in my bones. Call it instinct. But I knew from the first moment I saw you, and when I saw you, I fell."

"Fell."

"Hard." She wanted to laugh at herself but she couldn't, not after spending the last six months caught somewhere between hell and purgatory. "I knew then you were it. Everything. You were what I wanted. Heart, body and soul."

"And now?"

The tears filled her eyes, burning hotter than before but she fought to hold them back. "You're the last thing I need, but I suppose I had to come here this weekend to see it for myself. Had to come and say goodbye my way."

"You have a funny way of saying goodbye," he said, walking slowly, deliberately toward her.

"Horrible, isn't it?"

"Very." Clasping the back of her neck, he brought her to him, drawing her close, so close that there was no space between them, just contact, sensation, from head to toe.

"Goodbyes like this are dangerous," he added, tilting her head back with the pressure of his hand. His lips touched the wild pulse beating at the base of her throat. "They're like fire."

She shuddered, feeling feverish. "So I'm learning."

She felt his lips return to the pulse, the sensation razor hot. Incredible. Excruciating.

"You're usually a quick study, *bella*," he said, his mouth moving with tormenting slowness across her throat. "Makes me think you want to be burned."

Yes, she answered silently, shuddering at the feel of his body against hers.

Yes, she wanted fire, she wanted the burn if only to remember—relive—what it had once been like, how amazing it had felt to be taken by him.

He had to know she craved the feel of him, the weight of him on her, the hard, heavy pressure, the way he filled her, the way he stormed her world and made it his. She'd never known anything like the glorious sensation of being touched, possessed, and maybe it wasn't love but it was heady, seductive, intoxicating.

And then his mouth covered hers and it was so fierce, so demanding that something inside her snapped and she felt close to breaking, felt as though she needed to throw a white flag, cry surrender.

His hands were wrapping around her arms, sliding up to her shoulders and then down, molding her through the thin white slipdress with his palms, shaping her breasts, her rib cage, her torso before one palm returned to her breast.

His kiss sucked the hiss of pleasure from between her lips, and as his fingers worked her breast, cupping, pressing hard against her nipple. The rhythmic kneading, squeezing, rippled through her, bringing memory and desire to life. She shifted, brushing her hips against his, her body blindly seeking what it had so desperately missed.

Sex.

Dominance.

Surrender.

Surrender, she silently repeated as one of his hands slipped the strap of her gown down over her shoulder and he impatiently pushed the delicate fabric down to expose her skin.

She gasped at the heat of his hand against her skin, gasped again as he seemed to count and measure her ribs, a reclaiming of her body, a reminder of all that he'd given her, all that they'd experienced together.

And as his bare palm slid across her chest, his palm capturing her breast, squeezing her taut nipple, his control slipped, and he, too, cracked, and something primitive and wild took over.

He split the gown open down the back with one fierce tug of his hand, the zipper giving way, the fabric ripping wide-open. He stroked the length of her bare back until he came to the ivory satin garter belt hooked around her waist.

She felt his quick breath as his examination slowed, his fingers tracing the satin around her waist and the narrow satin stays that held her silk stockings high on her thighs.

He'd always loved her lingerie, loved the exquisite laces and silks, the satin panties, the delicate bras and bustiers.

He stroked the length of her, from the back of her neck all the way down to the small of her spine, stroking each skin, inflaming the nerves, stirring all the senses.

When she trembled against him he cupped her bottom, his palm so warm on her bare cheek, the tiny satin thong panty covering next to nothing.

How she loved the feel of his hands on her, loved the way he touched her, his fingers burning, kneading, branding her.

Branding her his.

Aggressively he moved her, lifting her off her feet to place her back down on the edge of the Florentine chair. She felt awkward perched nearly naked on the chair's edge with her torn gown bunched loosely around her but it was the way he wanted her, the way he intended her to sit for him.

He parted her thighs wider, his large hands on each of her knees, and he looked down at her and smiled faintly. "I've always loved to look at you," he said, holding her still and drinking his fill.

Then he knelt at her feet and moved between her thighs.

She jerked as his mouth touched her between her legs on the satin thong, the flimsy fabric already damp and clinging tightly to her heated body.

She wanted him. But she'd always want him. He knew it, too.

His mouth moved across the damp satin, teasing her, shaping it even closer to her body. She gasped, squirmed, legs trembling as the tip of his pointed tongue pressed hard at the apex of her thighs, finding the small rigid nub where all her nerve endings came together in intense, erotic pleasure.

Her hips shifted on their own accord, her hips grinding in a helpless dance, wanting more than just the tip of his tongue against the satin, wanting his tongue on her skin, wanting the feel of his damp tongue against her slick flesh.

"Maximos," she groaned as his palms slid across the inside of her thighs, slow, torturous caresses that stirred her senses but brought no relief.

But he ignored her hoarse plea, his thumbs instead skimming close to the edge of her thong, finding the hollows where her thighs joined her body, playing the nerves dancing beneath her skin. She felt like a puppet on a string, jerking, jumping with every touch of his hand and mouth. He was tormenting her with the pleasure but at the same time giving no relief.

And then with a practiced hand, he reached for the thong and with a quick movement, ripped the fabric wide-open, tearing it off her body, leaving her completely open to him.

Cass choked on a breath, skin flaming, cheeks burning as his dark head lifted and his narrowed, stormy gaze slowly traveled the length of her, taking in the fullness of her breasts, the rise and fall of her rib cage, the pale bones at her hips, and the thighs parted wide, exposing all of her to him. With his gaze on her face, he reached for her, strumming her dampness with his fingertips, watching her jerk and clench her muscles, watching her tense expression, measuring her response.

"Maximos," she repeated, grinding out his name, her voice so deep and husky that it sounded as if it came from someone other than her.

And this time he responded, leaning toward her, putting his mouth on her, his lips against the hot silk of her inner skin where she burned and melted and needed so much of him.

With his mouth against her heated skin, she quivered and reached for him, burying a hand deep into his crisp hair, hanging on to him as his tongue touched her, traced her, made her even hotter, wetter, made her want him even more.

Cupping her hips, he slid his palms beneath her bottom and tilted her up to him even as he tugged on the garter belt stays, allowing the satin stays to create friction against her skin.

So many sensations…so much to sweep her up, dazzle her…

His cool tongue on her hot slick skin, his fingertip testing her dampness, another of his fingers toying with the silk hose encasing her thigh. She dragged in air, her rib cage rising, falling, her body tightening at the endless pleasure.

And his mouth never left her, his mouth moving on her, tracing her, sucking her, making her feel far too much, making the sensation far too strong.

She arched against him as the pressure inside her grew, tension building, the climax becoming something tangible, something real.

Cass dug her hands into Maximos's hair, felt the hot sting of tears in her eyes, felt love, felt anger, felt the unquenchable fire of desire.

His mouth pressed closer, his fingers buried in her. He wasn't going to let her go, not without making her his, breaking her resistance.

She was, after all, his.

His possession.

His object.

His mistress.

His woman.

And she was there, at the peak, that pinnacle where sensation is so true, tension so tight that the only way to go is through. Through and over and into. Into the coil of feeling, of being, and she shattered even as his mouth held her, caressed her.

She would, she thought, giving herself over to him, always be his.

Maximos lifted her from the chair and carried her to the bed. The velvet bed coverlet rubbed at her skin as she lay back. Maximos followed, stretching out over her, his weight settling on her. Even though she'd just experienced the pinnacle of pleasure, she still wanted *him*, and the desire to be joined with him was intense.

"Are you protected?" he asked, making room for his body between her thighs.

"I'm still on the pill." Not that it had protected her last time. Not that Maximos would ever know. There were some things she'd carry with her to the grave.

Confident that they could safely precede, Maximos touched her, made sure she was ready for him, and of course she was. But even though she wanted him, it still hurt when Maximos entered her. He was big, hard, and taking him inside her had always stretched her, required a quick breath to help her adjust to his size. But tonight the sting of pain was already giving way to pleasure. The feeling was unreal, the sensation of him in her, filling her, taking her, so addictive and so familiar.

Something happened when his skin was on hers, his body in hers. She felt fierce, hungry, craven. With him in her, making love to her, she knew she'd do just about anything for him. Nothing was unthinkable. Nothing taboo.

And maybe that's how she'd fallen for him. Not for his kindness or his tenderness, but his skill in bed. Because making love with Maximos felt like love. When he touched her, covered her, she couldn't imagine anyone else touching her again. Couldn't fathom desire—need—pleasure with anyone else. Just once with Maximos had changed her forever.

Cass the Invincible would never have believed such a thing was possible.

Now with Maximos's body covering her, and his warmth penetrating her skin, she felt consumed by the hunger that had once raged inside her. They'd been together for over two years and the sex had never grown stale, the desire never waned.

Again, she'd silently begged, again. Again.

Again.

And he had, until the day she wanted more from him than his body. When she'd asked for his heart.

And that, she'd discovered, was the wrong thing to ask for.

The pain of remembering couldn't dampen the erotic pleasure he gave her now. Her body loved his, wanted him, and as Maximos surged into her in deep, powerful thrusts, she gave herself over to him yet again as they climaxed together.

Later, it was wordless silence, the night dark, the room still, the air thick with tension, with all that was unsaid. Because there was so much unsaid that couldn't, wouldn't, be spoken now. That would never be spoken now.

Lying there in the dark with Maximos next to her, Cass felt as if a massive weight lay on her chest and her throat was slowly squeezing closed. She couldn't breathe, not well, not easily.

She knew how this would end. Knew what was coming next. She dreaded what was coming next.

He'd get up, and leave.

She hated the leaving part, had always hated the leaving part but it seemed positively excruciating now.

What she should do was leave, right now. She shouldn't wait for him to get up, shouldn't wait for him to make the move. Instead she should be strong.

Cass swallowed, touched the edge of the duvet, preparing to throw it back. All she had to do was get up. Stand up. Yet her body wouldn't move, and she lay, inert, lay in silence and pain.

Making love again had ripped her wide-open all over again. Taken whatever thin covering lay over her wounds, peeling it off, leaving her even more bare and exposed than before.

Sex for him was a release.

Sex for her was love itself.

Cass felt Maximos stir beside her. He was going to leave. Panic rushed through her, the panic of leaving fantasy and returning to reality, the panic of knowing how bad she'd feel once he'd left, the panic of facing the pain—alone—of being alone after being with the person she loved most.

"Don't go," she whispered, putting her hand out, placing her hand in the middle of Maximos's chest. His heart beat so warm and steady beneath her palm. Something inside her knotted and she thought life had never been so beautiful and awful. "Stay. Stay with me."

She felt Maximos's indecision, felt the ripple in his muscles as he considered whether to get up or lay down again and she found herself repeating her plea. "Stay with me until morning. Please?"

He hesitated a moment longer and then he pressed against her palm, moving her hand out of the way. "Can't stay all night. There's too much for me to do still tonight."

The pain was almost too much. She took a quick breath, and another. Why had she come here? Why had she done this? She wasn't strong enough. Since losing the baby she wasn't strong at all…

"Maximos." She touched her mouth to his chest, kissing his warm still damp skin. "Another hour then. That's all I'll ask for. I promise."

"I'll have to go sooner or later."

She knew that. She knew how it worked. She felt like she was always robbing Peter to pay Paul. "Okay."

"Okay," he echoed before drawing her close, settling her slim body next to his. "For the next hour I'm yours."

Maximos felt Cass take a swift breath, heard the faint catch in her voice. "Mine for an hour," she whispered.

She was fighting tears.

Maximos felt a stab of remorse, regret for the things that couldn't be changed, regret that Cass had ever been hurt by their relationship because she had been hurt, very hurt, and it was the last thing he'd wanted.

From the beginning he'd tried to shield her from his life, from the reality that was, from the facts that couldn't be changed no matter how many times you looked at them.

From the beginning he'd wanted to protect her. She deserved

protection, deserved to be cherished. He knew about her past, knew her mother had been left, abandoned, and knew the one man her mother had fallen for years later had been unavailable. Emotionally. Spiritually. Legally.

Cass should never have been his mistress. She should have been someone's wife. Treasured. Respected. Valued.

Stifling the anger and self-loathing within him, Maximos drew her even closer, held her more securely and kissed the top of her head. *Not an hour,* he silently corrected. *Yours forever.*

CHAPTER SEVEN

DON'T look at the clock, Cass told herself, don't watch time pass. Because an hour was nothing. An hour was brutally short. Just sixty minutes. Three thousand six hundred seconds. An hour would be gone in no time.

And despite being held so securely, Cass felt pain at being in Maximos's arms, not joy. Because she was waiting again. Waiting to say goodbye, to let him go.

She hated waiting, too. Hated letting him go.

She could do a hundred things—all difficult, all requiring prowess, talent, skill. But the one thing she couldn't do was let Maximos go.

She'd tried, too. God knows she'd tried. She'd wanted more, needed more, but somehow less with Maximos seemed better than more with anyone else.

Now lying in Maximos's arms, curled against his side, Cass felt the past rise up, the life she'd lived and she was suddenly, vividly reminded of their last weekend together, the weekend in Paris which didn't turn out to be a full weekend at all. She'd arrived Saturday afternoon, was scheduled to fly out Sunday noon, and a car was waiting for her at the airport.

She took the car to her hotel—the Four Seasons, of course—and checked into her suite and waited.

And waited.

And finally he called late Saturday night—to say he couldn't make it, but he'd see her Sunday morning, he'd definitely see her before she returned home. She'd been upset, hurt, disappointed and yet she clung to the fact that he'd promised Sunday morning, held on to the fact he'd given her his word.

And he had come Sunday morning and they'd had a late breakfast before he'd taken her to the airport but it wasn't the weekend she'd hoped for.

Just like their relationship had never been what she'd hoped for. Because she'd needed more than empty hotel suites, even if they were lavish suites. She'd needed less disappointment and more peace. Less hurt and more happiness.

Maybe he did keep his word, because like that Sunday in Paris, he'd eventually show up but more and more often he'd show so late there was no time to talk properly, make love properly, be loved properly.

And now she'd let it happen again, and everything was screaming inside her, everything was on fire. She'd allowed herself to be reduced to nothing. Because she loved him.

It felt as if she'd carelessly cut her own throat and the knife hadn't even been that sharp, but she'd done it fast, surrendered herself to him before she thought her actions through. Before she understood the consequences.

Cass bit down on her tender knuckles. She'd been tricked, fooled by the body and the senses. Somehow, each time she made love with Maximos, she thought there was more. She was sure there was more…that there could be more, if she only asked.

If she dared to risk.

Because making love with Maximos made sense. She loved the way he looked at her. She loved the heat and the interest and energy. And when he touched her, the walls came down completely and it was about them, the two of them together. Sexy, seductive, and inexplicably beautiful. No one had ever touched her the way Maximos did, no one had ever made her feel so perfect. So…sacred.

In his arms like this, the only thing she feared was time. When he was with her, she feared time passing. When he was away, she feared time slowing. Time was the only obstacle.

Or so she'd once thought.

Maximos rubbed her shoulder, dropped a kiss on her head. "I have to go now."

"Max—"

"It's been an hour."

And they'd made a deal. She'd begged him to stay, and he had, and now she couldn't make him feel bad for leaving.

"All right," she said, her voice low and unsteady.

"You'll be okay?"

No. "Yes."

She felt him throw the covers back and he slid from the bed and then drew the covers back up over her.

"You're sure?" he asked, reaching for his clothes.

She listened to the clink of his belt buckle, the whisper sound of fabric sliding against skin. "Yes." But she couldn't watch him dress. She couldn't do it again so she closed her eyes, turned her head away. But the hurt was huge, sharp, a dragon with endless teeth. Why was he always leaving her?

Or was she just the kind of woman men left?

Cass hiccupped as the door quietly opened and closed.

He'd gone.

Maximos had made it perfectly clear tonight that he wanted no commitments, nothing to tie him down. She was, and always had been, about convenience.

And she wasn't convenient anymore.

Battling tears, she pulled the duvet up over her head, covering herself entirely. *Don't think*, she told herself. But the hot, humiliating tears wouldn't stop falling.

How could she have loved him so much and he felt so little?

How could he take her, make love to her, for two years giving her pleasure, receiving such pleasure, only to let it all go away?

How could he just walk away? She'd given him everything—access to all her body and every millimeter of her heart—why hadn't that been enough?

The questions burned her, returning now just to haunt her just as they had every night and day for the past six months. How could someone willingly give up something like what they had? Their relationship was different. Their desire was hotter, brighter, their satisfaction greater. They had *everything*.

How could that not be enough?

She sobbed into the crook of her arm, sobbing so hard there

were moments she couldn't catch her breath and finally she knew she had to stop. *Pull yourself together.* This isn't the end of the world. *You'll get over him. It's just a matter of time.*

Pushing wet strands of hair from her cheek, Cass took a deep breath, and then another. *Time heals all wounds.*

Maybe. Maybe not.

She drew a shaky breath, and then another. *This, too, shall pass. Nothing lasts forever.*

And yet the clichés just made her angrier.

She didn't want to get over Maximos. She didn't know how to get over Maximos. Not when she still wanted him like this, not when she still needed him like this. Not when she was still so deeply, hopelessly in love.

Maximos Guiliano, love of her life. Maximos Guiliano, father of the child she'd lost.

Cass woke the next morning to brilliant sunshine and the sunshine confused her, tricked her. For a moment she didn't know where she was or why she felt as though she'd been run over by a truck and left for dead.

And then it hit her. It all came back. What happened last night. Where she was today. Maximos's house. Maximos's guest room. The morning after…

The ache inside her was nearly intolerable. And the sunshine didn't help, she thought, rubbing tiredly at her eyes, her eyes sore from crying herself to sleep.

But it was a new day, and Cass forced herself up. Leaving the bed, she began gathering her clothes still scattered on the floor—the silk hose, the satin garter belt, the torn panties and gown. And there in the tangle of clothes Cass discovered Maximos's cotton undershirt, the one he'd worn last night beneath his dress shirt.

She picked up the cotton T-shirt and pressed it to her chest, still able to smell Maximos's spicy fragrance on the fabric.

Maximos. The heartbreak hit her again, the heartbreak still so stunning, always unreal. And pressing the shirt to her mouth, a kiss of sorts, she breathed in the scent of him, breathed in the emotion before tossing the shirt back to the ground.

In the ensuite, Cass stepped beneath the shower, let the water stream down washing away all memory of last night's lovemaking.

She dressed swiftly, not letting herself think, not letting herself feel.

She was on the stairs, carrying her suitcase down when a hard voice sounded in the stairwell. "Going somewhere, Cass?"

The sound of Maximos's voice behind her made her jump, and she jerked around on the step. "You scared me," she said, putting one hand on her chest to quiet the mad drumming.

He was dressed in khakis and a crisp olive-green shirt and with his dark hair combed and his jaw shaven smooth he looked coolly elegant and perfectly in control.

Unlike the man who'd taken her to bed last night.

Unlike the lover who'd made her so completely his...

Pain sliced through her and she held her breath, trying to stay calm, maintain control like Maximos.

"So where are you going?" he asked, eyes narrowing.

If she didn't think and just allowed herself to be, she could feel the heat and strength of Maximos's body against hers still. She could feel the way he took her. Loved her. If she didn't speak and didn't move she could smell his clean spicy scent, a combination of his amazing skin and expensive but subtle cologne. She could taste his mouth on hers, the warmth and the coolness of his tongue playing hers, his lips teasing hers, the scrape of his teeth, the bristles of his beard.

The sex worked so well. Why did nothing else?

Cass swallowed the lump filling her throat and shifted her suitcase from one hand to the other. "I'm going home."

He just looked at her, a long level look that made her insides curl. He was angry. Angry with her. "I guess you finally got the closure you needed."

"I did come for closure."

"Is that a polite way of saying you wanted to get laid one last time?"

She flushed. "That's not fair—"

"Then what was last night?"

"Don't act like last night was so meaningful for you. You couldn't *wait* to get out of there."

"I've a house full of guests. Responsibilities—"

"It's not just last night, Maximos. You never stay after you've finished making love. For over two years I asked you to stay, to spend the night with me, but each time you had to go. You always have excuses. But it's lonely being left. It feels awful watching you dress and go."

"So now it's your turn to walk out."

Defiantly she looked up, met his gaze squarely, reading the intensity in his dark eyes. He was still so hard. So fierce. He'd take her to bed again and again, but that was it. The extent of what he'd offer her. Outside the bedroom, he'd never give her more. He would take her body, pleasure her body, but he'd never love her. "Maximos, there's nothing for me here."

"There was plenty between us last night."

"That's called sex."

"It works."

It was exactly what she feared he'd say, what she didn't want him to say. She wanted him to want her, fight for her, crave her the way she craved him. And for the longest moment she couldn't speak because it hurt, this gap in needs, a difference that was now clearly insurmountable.

"I deserve more than sex," she said finally, a terrible lump filled her throat. "I deserve more from you."

"More?" He was toying with her, his tone downright mocking. "As in gifts? Trinkets? Tokens of my affection?"

Her jaw tensed, flexed. It seemed impossible that they'd been lovers for so long, that they'd actually believed their relationship worked.

How had so little been enough for her for that long? Cass couldn't imagine ever settling for less now, not when she knew that she'd had her priorities all wrong, that she'd never known herself, who she'd been, and what she'd needed. Sex might feel good, but she wanted love. Sex answered certain physical needs but it didn't satisfy the emptiness inside, the longing to be accepted, cherished, validated. "I've had enough trinkets and tokens. I'd like a real relationship, one based on trust and respect—"

"I trust you. And respect you."

"One where both people give." This was killing her, making all her frustrations and needs known. She hated being vulnerable like this, hated having to ask for anything. "You didn't give, Maximos, you took."

He shrugged. "I gave you what I could."

She gritted her teeth at his tone, hating his calm indifference, that insufferable arrogance which set him above her, making him the mature, rational one and she the emotional, needy female.

It seemed almost inconceivable now that she'd given herself to him so freely, that she'd allowed him such access to her body, as well as her heart, because she'd given him her heart, too, and it was the one thing he hadn't wanted.

Cass drew a rough breath. "Maybe I need to be completely honest. Maybe what I should say is that I don't understand how you could make my body feel so good, but care so little about the rest of me? What was so special about my body?"

"Cass."

"Don't Cass me. Don't make me feel bad for wanting more. There's nothing wrong with wanting to make love instead of just screwing." She felt so exposed now, so needy and vulnerable but she couldn't help it. It had all been pent up for too long. The wants. The needs. The fear.

Why couldn't he give her what she needed? Why couldn't he love her?

She was asking for love, not money, not power, not fame, nor success. Love.

"Maybe all I need is to screw." Maximos's deep voice, pitched low and hard, echoed in the hall.

"Great," she choked, grabbing her suitcase and heading down the stairs rapidly, one quick step at a time. "Get laid. Go screw. Just stay away from me."

"You don't mean that," he said, following her down the staircase. "Or you wouldn't have traveled all this way to see me again."

"I told you. I needed closure."

"Or another mind-blowing orgasm."

And then he laughed, and Cass stopped midstep, turned to face him. "You're making me hate you."

"Good. You should hate me. You shouldn't have ever accepted what I gave you." And he pulled her into his arms, pulled her against him so she felt the hard press of his body from his chest to his hips to the thigh he pushed between her legs even as his head descended and his mouth covered hers.

His kiss stole her breath, his mouth forcing her lips open, forcing her surrender. He knew what he wanted and he was determined to have it.

Cass shuddered at the flick of his tongue against her sensitive inner lip, shuddered again as he reached up to clasp the swell of her breast, his palm hard against her nipple, pressing, bearing down even as need coiled in her belly, fierce, sharp insistent.

Her legs trembled and helplessly she arched against him as he strummed her nipple, a pinching, squeezing sensation that tormented her nerves, heightening pleasure to almost pain.

She wanted him.

Now. Here. In her.

She wanted him. Hard. Fast. Furious.

She wanted him and she felt mindless, helpless, his. And he knew, he *knew*.

She'd give him anything he asked. She'd beg him to take her, fill her, beg him to give her release.

The pressure on her mouth eased and she drank in air as his head briefly lifted.

"You should have demanded more," he said, his voice rough, raspy with passion. "You should have insisted on more from the very beginning."

Her head was swimming, spinning, her senses stretched, teased, dazed. She felt empty, achy between her legs. And her heart felt just as empty, and achy in her chest. There would never be true release. Not from him, not with him. He was put on earth to torture her. "Why are you doing this?" she choked.

"Because you wouldn't. You couldn't. And it needed to be done. I was never any good for you, *bella*."

Her eyes stung. He was being awful, making the ending of this—whatever it was, whatever it had been—excruciating.

She couldn't bear for it to be awful. In fact, she wanted nothing more than to make everything okay. Closure for her meant making everything okay, but maybe this time there wouldn't be real closure. At least there wasn't going to be peace.

Because beyond the discomfort of the moment, beyond the pain, there was pride. And self-respect. As well as something called self-preservation.

If he wasn't going to help her, protect her, then she had to protect herself.

And if he couldn't respect her, she had to do that for herself, too.

Tears welled in her eyes and for a moment she felt lost. Abandoned. And it wasn't something she ever wanted to feel, not again.

No, she had to make sure she was safe. Valued. Treated well. She deserved to be treated well.

And those thoughts, those elusive rational thoughts allowed her to stand on tiptoe and kiss him, kiss him gently, tenderly, kiss him with pain and heartbreak before she broke away, descended the rest of the staircase and exited through the front door.

Maximos stood frozen on the step and watched her go.

He saw her walk through the door and shut it and as the door shut he felt a rush of emotion—mostly rage—before telling himself not to think.

Don't care.

Quickly he began to climb the stairs again, heading back to his room to change for the excursion Adriana had planned, and as he climbed the stairs he kept chanting don't think, don't care, don't feel. There was no point thinking or feeling now. What was, was. Period.

But Maximos knew he'd hurt her. Knew he'd leveled her, hitting her far harder than was fair, and it made him sick.

He didn't want her hurt. He didn't even know why he said what he'd said to her. He was angry, yes. And lashing out. But she wasn't the one he was angry with. No, his anger was directed at Sobato and Lorna, and the courts…at himself. But not Cass and yet now Cass was standing on the front steps of his house…

He should go to her. Apologize. Explain.

Reaching the top of the staircase, he drew a breath. But explain what? That he'd betrayed her? That he'd knowingly betrayed her for years? How could he explain? That he'd been as unfair to her as Lorna had been to him?

But Cass didn't know any of that yet. She didn't know about his real life, the life he'd kept hidden, private, the life that would crush her if she found out.

And she'd soon find out. He had to tell her. Last night he'd determined he'd tell her this weekend, as soon as the wedding was over and Adriana had set off for her honeymoon. It was time. But until the wedding he wanted to keep the drama low…for his family's sake if nothing else.

Inside his bedroom, Maximos stripped off his shirt and searched through his bureau for another.

His bedroom door opened abruptly. "Maximos." It was his mother.

"You don't knock?" he asked, turning to face her.

"I'm your mother."

"Which is why you should knock. You never know what you might find."

"Oh, I don't worry about you doing anything in your bedroom." His mother's face was impassive. "You do it on the stairs."

He shot her a dark glance, resignation tinged with humor. "You shouldn't be watching."

"Some things, Maximos, are hard to miss." His mother remained in the doorway, slim, elegant, very contained. She wasn't particularly tall and yet she exuded authority. Control. She hadn't been married to a Guiliano for nearly forty years for nothing. "Now your…guest…is outside with her suitcase. Does she have a ride?"

He slipped on a white linen shirt and began rolling the cuffs back. "I don't know."

"Why is she leaving now?"

"I'm not sure—"

"You are sure. You've just been fighting with her for the past ten minutes."

Maximos's brow lifted. "She needed to go back to Rome. Business."

"On a Saturday?"

"She's an advertising executive—"

"On a Saturday?"

"*Mama.*" His voice dropped, the tone low, a warning.

"Adriana said she was Emilio's girlfriend," his mother continued unabashed. "But she's not, is she? She's yours."

"She couldn't be my girlfriend—"

"I'm not stupid, Maximos. I'm your mother, and I've known you longer than two or three years. I know what I heard, and I know what I saw. She doesn't know the truth, does she?"

He said nothing, his jaw tight.

Signora Guiliano took a step forward, her expression just as fierce as her son's. "At least tell her the truth. Maybe she'll think you're selfish, instead of simply cruel."

"Thanks." His sarcasm wasn't lost on her.

She shot him a piercing look before heading to the door. "At least get her a ride back to Rome. No taxi will take her back today." And she walked out without looking back or saying goodbye.

Maximos stood a moment listening to his mother's footsteps echo down the hall. Nothing like an overbearing Sicilian mother, he thought, but the corner of his mouth quirked. He loved her. Strong women had never intimidated him.

Cass was standing next to her suitcase on the palazzo's broad stone steps when the front door opened and Maximos appeared. He'd changed into a casual white linen shirt and khaki shorts.

"Going somewhere?" he asked, standing next to her.

"Yes."

His expression was quizzical. "How do you intend to get there?"

Cass felt sick on the inside, sick and shaky and she wished she'd never come here, wished she were in Rome where she belonged but she'd leave soon. As soon as she had transportation. "A taxi."

"No taxi will drive you back to Rome on a Saturday. It's an all day trip. You'll need a hire car. Have you reserved one?"

He knew she hadn't. "No."

"That poses a problem."

She tucked a strand of hair behind her ear but refused to look at him. What did he want her to do? Beg? "You could loan me one of your cars."

"I couldn't. Insurance issues and all."

"I'm a good driver. Accident free for over ten years."

"It's nothing personal, Cass—"

"Nothing personal? You will sleep with me, but not loan me a car?"

"I've had difficulties with car insurance due to an accident a number of years ago. You can ask my mother, or my sisters if you don't believe—"

"I don't want to ask them. I just want to go." Her fingers gripped the suitcase handle tightly.

She'd been so impulsive coming here. But then she'd been a gambler her whole life, a player in the game, confident, bold, aggressive. She'd taken risks in her personal life just the way she'd taken risks in business, but this time, she'd failed.

Failed. Cass blinked back tears thinking that until Maximos entered her life, she'd never failed at anything. "I don't know what I was thinking...don't know what I thought would really happen."

"Maybe you thought I'd see you and remember how much I enjoyed being with you and we'd get back together."

The tears grew hotter, filling her eyes completely. "Please stop."

"You came for answers, Cass."

She had to turn her face away, not wanting him to see the tear sliding down her cheek. "I think I got them."

"Are you sure you got the right answers?"

There was the strangest note in his voice, a tone akin to suffering but it couldn't be. This was Maximos after all. And he didn't feel, and he certainly didn't suffer. But before she could answer the front door was flung open and Adriana came racing out of the house in a short skirt and bathing suit top.

"Maximos!" Adriana cried, hugely vexed. "What are you doing? We're all waiting on you and you know we can't set sail without you. What's the problem?"

Then Adriana spotted Cass and her expression changed. The look she gave Cass was pure malice. "Are you waiting for Emilio to pick her up?" Adriana asked tersely.

Maximos shook his head. "Emilio's gone." He paused. "And Cass isn't with Emilio. She's with me."

Cass's head jerked up. Adriana looked equally stunned.

The corner of Maximos's mouth tilted. "I've been seeing Cass for over two and a half years."

CHAPTER EIGHT

ADRIANA looked from Maximos to Cass and back again. "*You've* been seeing her?"

"Yes," Maximos answered.

"Not Emilio?"

"No."

Adriana's forehead creased. "Then why did she arrive with him?"

Maximos's jaw tightened. He hesitated for just a fraction of a second but Cass's stomach knotted anyway. "To surprise me," he answered smoothly.

Adriana looked suspiciously from one to the other. She seemed to be trying to make up her mind about something. "You didn't seem happy to see her yesterday."

"You know how I feel about Sobato."

"Mmm." Adriana's lips pursed and then with a glance at Cass and her suitcase, asked yet another question. "Why is she leaving now then? Why before the wedding?"

"Something came up." He saw his sister's expression and he shook his head. "It's complicated—"

"Then uncomplicate it," Adriana retorted impatiently. "Because everyone's already on board and if we don't leave soon we won't be back in time to get ready for the ceremony."

Cass opened her mouth to speak but Adriana wagged her finger. "No. This is my day. I want you both to come now on the boat and share the picnic and make my wedding day happy." She looked at her brother. "Maximos cannot upset me today and I know him. If there is a problem, it's his problem. He's a typical man. He has too much pride."

Adriana tapped her watch. "Five minutes. You must be on the boat in five minutes." And with a fierce nod she marched away.

"You better go," Cass said quietly. "It is her day and she shouldn't be upset."

"Then you better come, too, because she said she wanted us both to go on the picnic."

"I'm not in a picnic mood," she answered, unable to hide her bitterness.

"Neither am I." His voice was brusque, forceful. "But there's no car coming for you, and unless Sobato is waiting somewhere for you, you're not leaving Ortygia anytime today. So you might as well join the outing and make the best of it."

"Is Sophia going to be there?"

He sighed, a long drawn-out exasperated sigh. "Sophia is not my girlfriend, and I have now publicly declared you my girlfriend in front of my family."

Cass lifted her chin. "But have you told your family you only want me for sex?"

His brow furrowed, his dark gaze brooding. "Cass—"

"I want to go."

"I'm sorry, Cass—"

"Fine. Apology accepted. Can I leave now?"

"No." But he said it softly, so softly it forced her to look at him, really look at him, and his expression surprised her because he looked lost. Confused. And despite her anger and hurt she couldn't walk out, not like this. "We need to talk. There are things we ought to discuss. Things you should know."

"Then tell me now."

"I don't want a scene before Adriana's wedding."

"What you're going to tell me will cause a scene?"

He hesitated. "It will be upsetting."

His tone scared her. "What? You're married?" She attempted to joke, needing to lighten the mood, needing laughter. But when she saw his shocked expression her laughter subsided. "I'm sorry. I was trying to add a little humor. But that's not funny. I know it's not funny."

His expression changed yet again, shifting, hardening, his features becoming closed and unreadable. For a moment there was just silence then he muttered something, shook his head.

"Stay for the rest of the weekend," he said. "Join us on the picnic, attend the wedding with me tonight and we'll talk in the morning once everyone departs." He paused, his gaze searching her face. "And you know we need to talk. We both need understanding…or whatever you think closure is."

Closure. Her favorite word. And she didn't want closure, she hated the very word, but she did need to understand what it was tearing them—and her—apart. She needed to do it for her. "Okay."

He smiled, but she didn't see relief in his eyes. If anything he seemed…resigned.

A few minutes later with shorts, swimsuit and sunscreen jammed into a woven bag, Cass walked with Maximos from the palazzo through town to the harbor where the boat waited.

But it wasn't just a boat, Cass discovered, as they reached the small port dominated by one luxurious yacht. The sleek, stylish Guiliano yacht was a ninety footer, built in Viareggio, Italy, its sophisticated design practically an art form.

As Adriana had said, all the wedding party and guests had already boarded the yacht by the time Maximos and Cass arrived at Ortygia's harbor. A lavish breakfast buffet had been prepared for the guests and the upper deck was a lively hub of activity as everyone milled about sipping champagne and balancing plates piled high with fresh fruits, sliced meats, cheeses and warm fragrant breads.

Maximos assisted Cass in boarding. "There's coffee, juice, plenty to eat," he said. "You'll want to have a good breakfast now as it'll be a number of hours before we arrive in Catania where we'll disembark."

"Is that where we'll have lunch?"

"At the castle at Aci Castello." Maximos signaled to the captain that they were ready to go. "If you'll excuse me a minute, I should greet the others."

He left her but he hadn't forgotten her. A ship steward appeared shortly at her side with a cup of coffee laced heavily with milk and a small plate with a croissant and cheese. Her favorite breakfast.

She glanced toward Maximos who was making the rounds, playing the cordial host, and her lips curved ruefully. He confounded her. She honestly didn't know what to make of him. Even here with his family he was so contained, so detached, essentially a closed book.

But why?

What made him mistrust so much? What made him want sex, but not love? Convenience, not commitment?

Why would a man as strong, as wealthy, as powerful as Maximos be so…afraid?

Now the yacht was pushing back from the harbor, motoring slowly past ancient Ortygia's striking stone buildings, and Cass's attention was caught by the buildings gleaming ivory and yellow in the wash of morning light.

She didn't think she'd ever seen anything so beautiful as the dazzling displays of architecture set against the brilliant turquoise water. Gold and sapphire, lapis and silver. Breathtaking.

The yacht reached open water and picked up speed and Cass remained at the ship's railing, watching the land recede.

"Would you like more coffee?" Maximos asked, joining her.

"Your steward's very conscientious. He's been by three times with fresh cups."

"That's what he's paid to do." Maximos rested his forearms on the railing, and he stared out at the bright blue water surrounding them. The morning was already quite warm and yet the breeze cut the heat.

Cass glanced at him over her shoulder. "Your sisters have been whispering and staring at me."

"You're beautiful."

She made a face. "That's not why they're staring at me."

He laughed, lifted his hands. "I'm sorry. You're right. You are beautiful but that's not why they're looking at you. They're curious."

"About…?"

"You. I've never…brought anyone here before."

"Never?"

"Not since I was a kid."

Maximos saw the way she looked at him, and he knew she didn't believe him, or maybe it's that she didn't understand him. Well, he couldn't blame her. He didn't understand himself.

All his life he'd thought he was one person and then he'd discovered he was someone else.

He'd always been strong, fair, just. But ever since meeting Cass…

He'd done nothing but play dirty. Break every rule.

"I'm glad you didn't go," he said after a moment. "I didn't want you to leave like that."

"But you know I'm going to leave. I have to."

He heard the cool note in her voice. She was still upset with him. She should be.

"Eventually, yes," he answered.

He saw her throat work and he felt a rush of inexplicable emotion—need, pain, anger, again, so much anger—and it was just a matter of days…hours…now before he told her the truth.

His gut churned knowing she'd be devastated. She'd never forgive him. Why would she forgive him? He couldn't forgive himself.

And this is why he'd ended it six months ago, he reminded himself. This is why he'd let her go. It was better for her. Cleaner. Smarter. Safer.

For her. And him. But mainly her.

How could she move on if she were still so emotionally tied to him?

Her hands balled on the railing. "You make me crazy," she whispered. "You pull away when I need you, come to me when I don't. You hurt me, and confuse me, and I don't know why I still care for you so much when you've made my life a living hell." Her voice broke and she dipped her head, hiding her face and Maximos knew she was trying not to cry.

If she were really his, he'd pull her to him and comfort her. But she wasn't his. Couldn't be his.

Cass knew Maximos was watching her, felt his ambivalence and his ambivalence just cut even deeper.

You have to be hard, she told herself, *tough*.

But she didn't feel hard inside, she felt like glass. She felt fragile…ethereal. Her strength and resolve were gone. It was as if the warrior had broken, leaving her crumpled. Leaving her so damn small.

She couldn't bear Maximos's anger or indifference any longer. She could take the brutality from anyone but him. She'd been his…how could he hurt her like this? How could he continue to be so cold, so hard, so removed?

What she needed most was tenderness. Now. Right now. She needed his arms around her, holding her, needed his lips against her neck, her cheek, her mouth, warming her, soothing her. Loving her.

But he didn't love her. And he felt no tenderness for her. He'd break her the same way he broke all his competition.

She pictured the luxury auto industry he'd so completely dominated these past ten years, recalled the sleek fast dangerous cars he'd perfected and realized he'd already broken her.

She was like one of his beautiful cars caught in a pileup. Twisted, crumpled metal marked by gritty piles of shattered glass.

Her head spun with the truth. She'd once thought she was so tough, so together. And yet now look at her…

She was nothing. She'd become nothing. Love had reduced her to this.

"Why do you still care?" Maximos asked after a long silence.

She made a rough sound in the back of her throat. "I loved you."

"Why?"

He wanted to discuss this here…now? He wanted a rational conversation *now*? He wanted to discuss love after six and a half months of torture?

Yes, she did love him but how could this be love? How could love hurt like fire? How could love level like this, smash, destroy?

She'd always been taught that love was patient, love was good. Love was kind. Love wasn't selfish.

But that's not how she felt. She felt angry. Fierce. And it was the waiting that had done this to her…to her heart.

The longing to hear from Maximos made every uncertainty roar to life, and when the silence stretched, when he didn't call, when the days and weeks passed without a word she felt her security slip, her peace of mind crack.

His distance left the door open to fear and doubt.

Was waiting this hard for everyone? Did other women feel this way when alone…did they wonder like she did? Did they worry? Doubt?

Did other women approach love with more confidence, with less fear?

If she'd felt deeply and truly loved would she have been more grounded, less nervous?

What would life have been like if she'd been his true love instead of a warm body in his bed?

And every time he left her, she prayed he'd say, *I'll call you.* And then she'd pray, let him call. Let him call soon. But he never did. He made her wait. And wait.

And slowly it broke her. It was the waiting for love that reduced her to this.

"Maybe it wasn't love," Maximos said, his shuttered gaze resting on her face. "Maybe it was lust and you thought it was love."

Her lips tugged, emotions sharp, too intense. "I know the difference," she whispered, thinking that the past seemed light-years removed, their volatile relationship part of someone else's life…someone else's experience, and even though the good feelings seemed so far away, she knew there'd once been good feelings in this relationship.

She looked at him, seeing his dark beauty, the hard lines and edges of Maximos Guiliano. Tall, powerful, authoritative. A Sicilian man who didn't compromise.

Her heart squeezed inside her chest. If only he'd compromised for her…

"I loved how I felt when I was with you," she said after a moment. "I loved how I felt when I looked at you. You gave me joy. You gave me peace. When I was with you I wanted nothing else, nothing more. Every moment was precious, every moment meant so much to me."

"Yet you never saw us in the future. You never saw us growing old together."

She looked at him strangely. "Why do you say that?"

Lines formed on either side of his mouth and for a moment he didn't answer. Then his head shook, his features tightening.

"I know I wasn't good for you, and I know I—and our relationship—had hurt you."

The relationship had hurt. After awhile. After the limitations had become too narrow, too restrictive, too binding.

"You didn't give me a future." She couldn't look at him anymore, the heartbreak back, the feelings so sharp and bittersweet. "You didn't allow me to dream. You made it clear from the start it was sex, and I tried to be content with sex."

She exhaled hard, and drew another breath, the air hot, aching inside her lungs. "But I fell in love with you anyway. I couldn't help it. You're not like anyone I've known before."

"You've been pursued by many successful men."

"It's not your success that makes you fascinating. It's you—your darkness, your complexity, your sharp edges. You're... dangerous, Maximos. And I know it. I've always known it."

"Danger's that attractive?"

She looked out over the deep blue water, trying to think of an appropriate answer, but all she saw was the ad campaign Italia Motors had hired her to do for their European market. The ads had been dark, moody, sexual. Nothing light or playful in the Italia Motors branding and she'd gotten that directly from Maximos herself.

One look at him and she wanted to slide out of her clothes and into close contact with him.

One night alone with him and she'd wanted every night with him.

"You're that attractive," Cass answered, ruefully. "You're that man every woman dreams about—the dark handsome stranger, the forbidden—and I wanted that."

"Forbidden."

She shrugged. "There's always an appeal to that which is out of reach, to that which we can't have."

"But you did get me. You did have me."

There was something in his voice, in his tone, that reminded her of how she used to feel when alone with him—desired, sheltered, adored. God, how she'd loved being with him, being loved by him. It was the best feeling in the world. "And I just wanted more." She tried to smile, but couldn't.

Maximos's forehead creased, deep lines furrowing between

his strong eyebrows and silence stretched between them, the silence stretching so long that Cass shifted. "I obviously shouldn't have wanted more," she added after a moment. "Me asking for more was the kiss of death, wasn't it?"

"There was nothing wrong with you asking for more." His voice was low, harsh. "I know you wanted more, needed more. I gave you very little." He hesitated, glanced at her, features savage. "I gave you virtually nothing."

He'd known.

Cass felt a flicker of pain, like the sharp edges of a palm frond brushing her heart, simultaneously cutting and caressing. He'd known.

She couldn't see, the sudden sting of tears blinding her vision and Cass gripped the railing, her head so full of words and emotions that she didn't even know where to begin.

How could love be so complicated?

As a child love had seemed so very simple. Emotion had been simple. You loved, you laughed, you hoped, you feared. Emotion had just been that—emotion. And you made your decisions based on honest emotion.

Then you learned.

You grew up.

You changed.

Love stopped being simple, direct, uncomplicated. Love became difficult. Dangerous. Complex. Love became something one could lose, something elusive and negotiable.

It became about behavior.

It became a reward.

It even became a punishment.

And for a moment Cass wanted nothing more than to be a child again with a child's innocence and the pure heart of one still young, still trusting. Because love was better like that, when one trusted, when one didn't worry and fear, when one didn't anticipate pain. When one didn't fear scrutiny never mind rejection.

Did anyone manage to grow up unscathed? Unscarred?

Did anyone reach adulthood—maturity—still trusting? Still centered? Still optimistic?

She wished she had. She wished she was more like the image

she projected, the one with impeccable suits, flawless hair, dazzling success. On the outside she looked like the perfect woman. But the perfection stopped there. Because on the inside she wanted so much more.

On the inside there was a woman who'd never felt secure, never felt loved, and she'd picked Maximos to love her because if he—difficult, untamable Maximos—should love her then she was truly valuable. Lovable.

"Can I just interrupt for a moment?" Annamarie, Maximos's middle sister, asked, joining them. She was cradling her infant daughter against her shoulder, one hand raised protectively to shield the baby's head and neck from the sun.

"Of course," Maximos answered, reaching to take his young niece from his sister. "I've wanted to say hello to this beautiful bambina all morning."

Cass couldn't watch Maximos with the baby. It was the last thing she wanted to see and she turned toward his sister who was looking at her with the strangest expression—surprised, as well as intrigued.

"I'm Annamarie," his sister said, introducing herself. "I'm sorry I haven't had a chance to meet you earlier. I think there was a misunderstanding—"

"It's okay," Cass interrupted, knowing what Maximos's sisters thought, and as it was what they were supposed to think, the last thing Cass wanted from any of them was an apology. "I understand."

"You're an American?" Annamarie asked.

"Yes."

"But you're Italian is excellent. I can hardly detect an accent."

"I hope so. I've lived in Europe for ten years now, five of those in Rome."

"You like Rome?"

"Very much so," Cass answered, tucking another loose strand of hair behind her ear. The yacht was moving at such a clipped speed that the deep blue water frothed with white foam. "It's become home."

"And Sicily?" Annamarie persisted. "Do you like it here?"

"It's my first visit."

"Your first visit? You mean Maximos has never brought you to his own country, to meet his own people before?"

"She's going to Catania and Aci Castello now," Maximos said calmly, gently patting the baby's back.

"But what about Agrigento, Palermo, Mount Etna?" Annamarie protested. "Those are all important to our culture. You can't possibly say you've visited Sicily if you haven't seen more."

"And I'd like to visit them," Cass said, wanting to change the subject, nearly as much as she wanted to escape. She couldn't handle seeing Maximos with the baby. It was too painful, too vivid of a reminder of what she'd lost. "Unfortunately I don't travel as much as I'd like. I tend to get preoccupied with work."

"Ah." Annamarie nodded with a glance at Maximos. "Another workaholic. I'm always saying to Maximos, don't work so much. You need to rest more, play more, but Maximos is very driven." Annamarie shot her brother another reproving glance. "He is not very good at taking things easy."

Cass smiled but she wouldn't meet Maximos's eyes. Instead her gaze dropped to the baby he was holding in his arms, the infant curled so contentedly against his chest, Maximos's powerful hand cupping the back of the baby's head, holding the infant easily, comfortably, cradling her as if it were the most natural thing in the world.

Her chest tightened with heartache. She and Maximos hadn't just had sex. They'd created life. They'd made a baby.

Their baby.

Cass watched Maximos return his niece to his sister, and the baby, dressed in a small pink outfit, crawled up Annamarie's shoulder, tiny hands grabbing at her mother's sparkly teardrop earring, studying the earring intently.

For a moment Cass couldn't breathe, pain shooting through her, a lance of white-hot heat. *That could have been me*, she thought, that could have been me with our daughter.

"What's wrong?" Maximos asked Cass as Annamarie walked away, excusing herself so she could feed the baby.

Cass looked at Maximos, but she didn't see him, just the ultrasound, that first glimpse of the daughter that wasn't meant to be. "Nothing," she said. "It's nothing." Because it was nothing now. Nothing she could do. Nothing she could change.

Even if she wanted to.

"You're not very comfortable with kids, are you?" he asked.

Turning her head away, she stared out at the horizon of blue, trying not to scream at the injustice of it. "I like kids."

She'd been thrilled she was pregnant. She'd been thrilled she was going to be a mother. Nearly thirty, it had felt right in a way she couldn't explain…not even to herself. She was ready to be a mother, ready for this next step in her life. Maybe she was too strong, too independent to make a good wife, but she knew how to love and her baby would be loved.

Then came the ultrasound.

She had a daughter.

And her daughter wasn't healthy. Nothing had come together quite right, limbs didn't attach correctly—a hole in her tiny heart.

Cass had been dumbstruck. The doctor talked. Cass stared at the sonogram. Her daughter—*her* daughter—wouldn't survive.

Sitting there in her robe, the cold gel drying on her stomach, time came screeching to a stop. After the doctor finally finished talking, she sat silent, her head buzzing with numbing white noise. And then the cloud cleared in her head and she was herself again. Tough. Determined. The fighter.

"How can I help her?" she'd asked.

The doctor's brow creased. He didn't speak. His expression grew more grim. "You can't," he said at last.

But it wasn't an answer she accepted. This was her daughter. Her daughter…and Maximos's. "There must be something." She strengthened her voice, and her resolve. "Procedures done in utero."

"It's unlikely she'll even survive birth. If she does, she won't survive outside of the womb."

Cass shook her head, furious. She wouldn't accept a diagnosis like that, and she'd stood then. Brave, fierce, undaunted. "You're wrong." Her voice didn't waver. "She'll make it. I'll make sure she survives."

But Cass had been the one wrong. Two weeks later she woke up in agony. Rushed to the hospital, she miscarried that night.

"Do you want a family?" Maximos asked, ignorant that each of his questions were absolute torture.

"Yes." Her eyes burned but she wasn't going to cry, couldn't cry about the devastating loss. Some pain went too deep, some pain caused insurmountable grief.

Losing Maximos had hurt—badly, badly—but losing their child had broken her heart.

CHAPTER NINE

IT WAS early afternoon when the picnic at Aci Castello ended with many of the Guiliano guests scattering to either explore the castle ruins or the beautiful beach at the foot of the *castello*.

It was hot, temperatures soaring for mid-September but Cass stayed with Maximos and his sisters who were stretched out on the blankets, their conversation light, teasing, punctuated with much laughter.

And Maximos teased his sisters as much as they did him. She'd never seen Maximos like this. She'd only ever known the proud Sicilian, the lover and warrior, never the man who cherished his family and was adored in return.

He lay not far from her now, propped up on his elbow. His body was powerful, muscular, beautiful. She tried not to stare and yet she couldn't not look.

His hand briefly touched his knee, his skin darkly tan, the hair on his thigh even darker, a crisp curling of hair on toned muscle, on taut bronze skin. She'd never met another man put together the way Maximos was. The ease with which he sat, he stood, he moved.

The shape of his head.

The perfect nape.

The broad palm, the strong hand absently stroking his knee.

Just looking at him made her remember last night, made her remember how it felt…skin on skin…his hand on her thigh…his hands everywhere. Watching him now she felt almost sick inside.

"Have you enjoyed today, Cassandra?" Adriana asked, sitting up and stretching.

Suddenly everyone was looking at her, and Cass, caught in the middle of thinking private thoughts, blushed. "I have, thank you."

It was true, too. She'd enjoyed her city tour of Catania, Sicily's second largest city, particularly the Roman Theatre uncovered in the 1860s as well as the Piazza Duomo dominated by the Cathedral, Town Hall and Seminary's exquisite Baroque architecture. But what fascinated her most, was the violent relationship Catania shared with the nearby volcano Mount Etna.

Since Catania's inception, it had been flooded with lava, rained on with ash, and completely destroyed in 1693 from a cataclysmic earthquake. When the city was rebuilt in the eighteenth century following the earthquake, most of the buildings were constructed from Etna's black lava.

"I just wish there was more time to explore. I'd love to visit Mount Etna itself," she added, and glancing up she saw that Maximos was watching her. He wasn't smiling, either. He looked hard. Focused. Intent.

What was he thinking? There was obviously something on his mind.

"What you must do the next time you come is take the Circumetnea Railway," Adriana said, cutting a wedge of cheese and snagging a small bunch of red grapes. "It's not a short trip, about five hours I think, but the train takes you on Etna's slopes through lava fields as well as vineyards."

"Sounds wonderful," Cass answered.

"So when do you think you'll come back?" Adriana asked, with an innocent look at Maximos.

"She hasn't even left yet," Maximos answered, extending a hand to Cass. "But it's probably time we all packed up and headed back to Ortygia."

Maximos helped Cass to her feet and after folding several blankets Adriana told Maximos that she and the others could finish up and so Maximos and Cass began a leisurely walk back toward the harbor.

"You're good with your sisters," Cass said as they left the others, walking through the tall sun burnt grass surrounding the ruins.

"Aren't most brothers?"

She shot a swift side glance. He looked calm, unflappable and perhaps that was the secret of powerful, aristocratic Sicilian men. Men like Maximos appeared impervious to storm, war and danger. Men like Maximos appeared to lack nothing and need no one. Men like Maximos were strong, forceful, invincible because they didn't let themselves feel, and they didn't expose themselves emotionally, physically. Risks were always anticipated, weighed, calculated. "I don't know. I was an only child."

"I never knew that."

She shrugged. "We never talked about our personal lives. Never discussed childhood, or our families."

They passed the *castello*, the sun drenching the stones of the ruins, the intense sun playing over the lava rock, patterning the stones shades of gold and bronze.

"Your parents?" he asked now.

"Divorced. They separated when I was fairly young."

Cass drew a sharp jagged breath, breathing in the warm air fragrant with sweet dry summer grasses. "Your father passed away a number of years ago, didn't he?"

"Thirteen years ago. I'd just turned twenty-five."

Cass glanced up at Maximos. "Were you close?"

"Yes."

Maximos's dark, watchful gaze rested on her face. "Were you close with your father?"

She hesitated a split second, trying to see her father's face, trying to remember something of him other than her mother's tears when he left. "No." She tried to smile, the grown-up smile of one coming to terms with the past, but it wasn't easy. Even now, after all these years. "He left us when I was still in school. He never came back. I…" She drew a breath and pressed on. "I never saw him again."

Maximos stopped walking. "You've never seen him again?"

She felt that odd pucker of pain in her heart, the kind of pain that's old, not fresh, a pain that has been part of you so long it's merely a scar you remember your old self by. "No."

"How could he leave you?" Maximos asked so gently, so quietly that tears pricked her eyes.

You did, she almost said, but she bit back the words, looked away, gazed out at what was left of the *castello*.

You could almost feel the ghost of the past here, she thought, stepping up onto a fallen stone. The air felt thick, saturated by time and the civilizations come and gone. The weight of time made her realize how insignificant she was. She might want to feel big and important, but no one lived forever. Not even the great leaders and philosophers lived forever.

She'd be gone before she knew it, that they'd all be gone and maybe this was the secret of places like Sicily, maybe this was what allowed the Sicilians so much passion and intensity. You only had today. So you had to live today.

"You're so good with your family," Cass said, her voice faint in the warm breeze. "Didn't you ever want to get married?"

Maximos's expression was shuttered. "You don't have to be married to be happy."

"Did I ever make you happy?"

"Yes."

"But you were afraid of committing to me?"

"I was never afraid of a girl like you," he answered, his voice deepening, his features hard, chiseled.

"A girl? I'm thirty, Maximos!"

"You might be thirty, but you're still a little girl on the inside."

His words made her heart ache. He made her remember who she'd been as a child, how she'd tried to assume the role of the adult, the parent, for her mother's sake. Her mother had never been able to cope after her father left and it was Cass's job to patch things up, to get things done.

"I can see the little girl in your eyes," he added, and the gentleness in his voice nearly undid her. "You're waiting for someone to come home."

"Please," she whispered, looking away, "I don't—" She broke off, licked the inside of her lower lip, her chest heavy with emotion. "I'm not. Not anymore." She turned her head, fixed a steady gaze on him. "I've learned."

"Learned what?" he asked, studying her just as intently.

She remembered the last six months, the sorrow at losing Maximos, the grief over the miscarriage, the deep sadness that didn't seem to go away. She'd fall apart, repair herself, patching herself together to get to work, accomplish a few things, but before she knew it, she'd be falling apart again, sitting at her desk with the glorious view of Rome and be fighting for survival.

Struggling to not drown.

Battling to keep her mind sane.

She didn't know how not to miss Maximos. Didn't know how to stop loving someone who'd become the only family she'd known in years.

When he left her it was like death but he hadn't died. If they'd been married, people would call it a divorce. But she wasn't his wife.

She was nothing. And she became nothing. And she'd learned nothing from the pain but not to want or need anyone again.

"Learned what?" he repeated.

She gave her head a slight shake, trying to chase away the dark clouds in her head, the memories that never got easier. "All things are possible." She swallowed the lump in her throat, met his gaze calmly, praying he didn't see the sheen of tears in her eyes. "I can bear all things."

He swore softly and reached for her, wrapping an arm around her, bringing her firmly forward until she was against him. Hip to hip, knee to knee, he completely dwarfed her, his body taller, bigger, stronger. And standing so close, she felt the tension running through him, as well as that thread of hot emotion, the emotion he didn't like, didn't want, but couldn't seem to control now that it was loose.

His head dropped, and she turned her face up to his even as his face dipped, his lips brushing hers. From anybody else the kiss would have been so brief she would have said it was nothing, but that slight caress of his mouth on hers was hot, sharp, fierce and her stomach tightened, legs trembling a little at the shock of it all.

His gaze followed the path of his lips, the fiery dark depths touching her lips, and then the pulse at the base of her throat. "That's a terrible lesson to learn," he mouthed against her throat, his voice deep, rough, a husky edge that made her feel far too much.

She wouldn't cry. There was no reason to cry now. "But practical."

"Practical." He said the word as if it amused him. "Practical, sensible, Cassandra. No wonder you've been so incredibly successful."

Cass stepped away from his arms. The warmth of his body weakened her defenses. She was far better standing apart from him, on her own two feet and swiftly she dropped her sunglasses back onto the bridge of her nose, concealing her eyes. *"Sensible?"*

"It's not a bad word."

"No, but…" Her lips pursed as she considered the past several years, her history with Maximos, and she shook her head regretfully. They might know each other's bodies, but they didn't understand each other's minds and hearts. "When have I ever been sensible?"

"At work. With your accounts."

Cass laughed softly. "You don't know me very well, do you?"

He plucked the sunglasses from her face, pocketing them. "Better than most, I'd say."

"Then if you know me so well, you should know I'm anything but sensible." She looked up at him, squinting against the sun. "What makes me good at work is that I'm daring, not sensible. I don't play it safe, Maximos. I never have. I've won awards because I'm not just creative, I'm a risk-taker. When other people pull back, I go for it. Where others play safe, I aim for the jugular."

She lifted her hand to shield her eyes, the sun reflecting brilliantly off the rocks of the ruins. "But I thought you knew that about me. Thought that was one of the things you—" and she drew a quick breath "—liked about me. But along with other things, I've discovered I was wrong."

"Not that wrong."

A brutal lump filled her throat. "Yet you didn't like me. Not as much as I'd thought." She fought hard to swallow.

"You're wrong about that, too." His mouth curved, the corners lifting in a crooked, self-deprecating smile. "I liked everything about you."

I liked everything about you.

Undone, she averted her head, the warm breeze lifting a loose tendril of her hair, blowing it across her face but Cass couldn't be bothered to tuck it behind her ear.

If only she could go back in time. She wanted the old Cass back, the one that was firm, strong, decisive. That Cass would know what to do now. That one would be able to handle all these conflicting emotions.

What had changed her so much? What had shattered her confidence?

Slowly, unsteadily, she tucked the loose tendril of hair behind her ear.

She had wanted more, so much more from him, and she didn't even know how to ask for more—she'd never asked for more from anyone—and he never volunteered it.

The truth was, at work she was aggressive, she knew what she wanted, she went after what she wanted, but at home…it was something else entirely. At home she wasn't sure about the rules. How did one get more? How did a woman get what she needed?

Was she to *ask*? *Demand*? Was it overstepping her boundaries to express what she needed?

"You say that now," she said, trying to keep her tone light, trying to cover what he did to her. And her heart.

"But facts disagree."

He shot her an assessing glance. "Maybe you never had all the facts."

"And what are those facts?"

Maximos regarded her for a long silent moment, the hot sun beating down overhead, the dry grass of the field biting at Cass's ankles. "I was a fan of your work for three years before you were signed to handle Italia Motors' new European ad campaign. I hand-selected you to manage our account, and was determined to have you no matter what the cost." He hesitated, his dark gaze settling on her face. "And I loved your mind before I even knew you had a face and body."

She said nothing, not knowing what to say.

"I can tell you about your biggest campaigns before we signed you," Maximos continued. "The campaign for PUMA and Tag Heuer. The stunning ads for GC distillery, they were my favorite—so bold, so dramatic and yet emotional. Your vision and ability to deliver won me over."

He paused, expression shuttered. "And then I met you, and you were even more incredible in person. I never had any intention of sleeping with you. But that night we finally met in New

York I knew I'd never meet anyone like you again. You were…perfect."

Her eyes burned. She ground her teeth together. She wanted her sunglasses, needed her sunglasses, needed to cover her face because she felt completely exposed. "So perfect you left me when I told you how much I loved you."

"No. So perfect I knew you would be much better off without me."

"That's bullshit." Anger rushed through her. Anger and hurt and defiance. "That's a cop-out. You don't care for someone and then push them away because they're what…perfect? Christ, Maximos! You broke my heart. You broke me. Why? Because I was so *perfect*?"

She walked away from him as fast as she could before the tears could have a chance to well up. She wasn't going to fall apart, not now, not any more.

Maximos was one of those men who for whatever reason couldn't commit. One of those men who loved but was afraid to risk, afraid of being hurt. He was the kind of man who'd always find a reason why things couldn't work out.

She didn't want that, didn't need that.

And all of a sudden she understood. All of a sudden she *knew*. It was so simple. It made so much sense.

She'd only come here this weekend to prove a point. Not to him. But to herself. Her. Oh my God. How ridiculous was that?

Cass dragged a hand through her hair, shocked. She'd come to Sicily determined to get Maximos back, determined to win him over despite the hurt, the rejection, the pain because she needed to prove she was lovable.

She needed to prove she wasn't easy to forget.

Needing to prove she wasn't her mother, and wasn't going to be left like her mother, and wouldn't be destroyed the way her father had broken her mother, or misled by her mother's lover who behaved as if he were single but actually had a family stashed away elsewhere…

Cass, the pragmatic kid who'd taken charge of her mother's shattered world, who believed she'd be smarter than her mother, and stronger, had in the end been her mother. In love. Out of love.

She'd picked a man that was nothing short of unavailable—and maybe he wasn't married like her mother's lover, Edward—but here she was, trying to make Maximos want her…need her…love her…even when it was obvious he couldn't.

He wouldn't.

Amazing.

Amazing. Cass could leave America behind, build a powerful career in Europe, become stunningly successful and yet she'd still been compelled to act out the pain and rejection of her childhood.

Would she have loved him so intensely if he'd been more available?

Would she have endured so much loneliness and shame if he'd been someone else…someone steady, permanent, available?

For that matter, had she ever fallen in love with someone available?

Had she ever fallen in love with someone who actually loved her?

No.

It had always been one-sided. It had always been unrequited, as if love had to be sharp and love had to cut. Love, the ruthless, Love the critic, Love the judge.

Her eyes burned nearly as much as her chest. What on earth had she been thinking all these years? What choices had she been making?

The insight stunned her. Horrified her. Made a mockery of her so-called independence and strength. She wasn't strong. She was destructive, self-destructive, spending her adult years trying to justify the pain of an eight-year-old who watched Daddy pack his bags and walk away.

What the hell was she trying to do with Maximos?

Make him return to her, make him come back so he could give her what her father never did? So he could save her—release her—from her father's curse?

Cass was suddenly stopped in her tracks, Maximos clasping her arm and dragging her frenzied march to a halt. "Leave me alone!" she choked, tears not far off.

"I can't."

"Why not? You did for the past six months! You let me go,

you didn't call or come see me. You let me go and you let me suffer. Endlessly."

"It's what you wanted."

"To suffer?" She laughed, feeling slightly hysterical. "Obviously I did if I stuck with this tortuous relationship so long." And the tears started to fall even as her heart burned, fire in her chest because she had suffered. She had. And he hadn't helped her, hadn't been there for her, hadn't reached out to her even when she needed him most.

"I never wanted you to hurt, Cass," he said, and the concern in his voice made her even more upset. "Maybe I haven't explained myself well, but I do care, and have cared—"

"About sex!"

"About *you*." He reached for her, drew her toward him.

Cass resisted. "If you cared about me, you would have talked to me, listened to me, supported me—not thrown me away." She tugged hard, struggling to pull away. "People aren't disposable, Max. I shouldn't have been disposable."

"It was complicated, Cass—"

"Excuses! I don't want excuses. And I don't want you to touch me. Not anymore. Because it's not fair…not fair how you use me…my body, my feelings…against me." And she broke free from him even as her senses screamed for more. She didn't want space. She wanted love.

Cass reached the yacht where everyone was boarding and took one of the last available seats on deck, a small chair in the shade and rubbed her temple, rubbed at the thick numb sensation banding her forehead.

She had to go.

She had to stop this nonsense and begin repairing the damage she'd inflicted on her life.

Maximos was the last to board. He waited until the yacht had set sail to approach Cass and silently he gave her the sunglasses back.

"Thank you," she said stiffly, sliding the sunglasses onto the top of her head, the glasses holding her long hair back from her face. She was so angry with him. She'd tried so hard to be what he needed, wanted, and what did he do? How did he make things easier?

He didn't. He did nothing.

And it wasn't until the glasses were on her nose, shielding her eyes that the strangest thought popped into her head.

Who was doing his new ad campaign? Because she obviously wasn't. She hadn't known Italia Motors had a new car about to be unveiled…which meant Italia Motors had gone elsewhere for the new car's advertising…

"Did you fire us?" she asked suddenly, rising, and reaching for the back of the chair to steady herself.

His expression immediately grew wary and the caution in his eyes pushed her over the edge. "No one at Aria Advertising knows about the new design," she said, "but if the new car's being unveiled soon you must have someone working for you."

He hesitated for a fraction of a second. "We do."

She stared up at him, shocked. Flummoxed. "Why?"

"I thought it best to go elsewhere."

"Why?"

"You know why."

"No, I don't, Maximos. Business is business. Your account at Aria Advertising had nothing to do with me."

He leaned toward her, his voice dropping so no one else could hear. "You had everything to do with getting our account—"

"So you yank it?" She didn't care if others heard. She was hurt. Outraged. Cass had always prided herself on being professional, working hard, no matter the cost. "I want more from you personally, so you punish me professionally?"

He took her arm, tugged her away from the lounge chairs, drawing her to the far end of the deck where no one congregated. "I was not punishing you. I was trying to help you."

She twisted her arm free, glared up at him. "Help me," she repeated fiercely.

"I knew you were having difficulties at work."

"No."

He crossed his arms over his chest, his skin burnished golden against his crisp white linen shirt. "I know how many companies are pulling their accounts—"

"So you do, too?"

"I thought perhaps you were under too much stress."

She exhaled in a painful whoosh. She couldn't believe it. Couldn't believe she'd lost another account—and not just any account—but Maximos's. If that wasn't the ultimate lack of confidence vote, she didn't know what was.

She turned away, stared out at the water. "When were you going to tell me?"

"A registered letter was delivered to the office yesterday."

But she wasn't at the office yesterday. She was en route to Syracuse, traveling with Emilio. "So everyone at the office knows." Her voice came out faint.

"I've had a call from Umberto."

Umberto being Aria Advertising's president and owner. "I bet you did." She suddenly felt chilled despite the warm day. Cass rubbed her arms lightly. Umberto would be livid. He'd want to blame someone, punish someone. That someone would be her. How ironic. She was here fighting for a relationship even as she was losing her job. "I wouldn't be surprised to find a termination letter waiting for me in Rome."

Maximos didn't immediately speak. His shoulders lifted imperceptibly and Cass felt rather than saw his sigh. "Umberto did say you'd had difficulties concentrating at work these past several months. He is concerned."

She could feel the weight of Maximos's gaze, could feel his concern and it made her furious. He had no right to be concerned. He'd not only walked away from her (because she just might be too perfect) but then he'd pulled his account, a massively important account, launching her into spectacular unemployment.

Wasn't life just wonderful?

"Cass." Maximos wasn't going to let her off the hook. "What happened?"

Little stars spun before Cass's eyes. She balled her hands into fists, air curdling in her lungs. What happened? What happened? She turned on her heel to face him. "*You* happened, Maximos. You were like a bloody Roman general. You came, you conquered and you went. And when you left, I had to pick up the pieces of my heart and it wasn't easy."

She drew a breath, eyes smarting but strangely dry. "You

changed me and my life whether or not you're willing to admit it. And you can take your account and give it to whoever the hell you want to, because I'm done with you. Done. Finished. *Fini*."

CHAPTER TEN

THEY were really good fighting words. Unfortunately she couldn't back them up quite yet with Maximos refusing to let her leave before the wedding. They argued all the way from Ortygia's harbor to the Guiliano palazzo, and continued their fiery debate all the way up the palazzo staircase.

"I do not have appallingly bad manners," Cass shot back at him, reaching her room with nothing short of delight. Hurrah! She could finally escape Maximos. "You're the one that dominates and dictates and refuses to compromise, much less capitulate."

"Capitulate? I'd never capitulate."

"Why not?" she stormed. "Because you're a man?"

"Exactly."

They were both breathing hard, tempers flying and Cass was not about to back down. "If you loved my mind so much, if you thought I was so talented why didn't you ask me if I could handle the pressure? Why go behind my back—"

"I didn't go behind your back. I simply responded to the rumors—"

"Rumors! That's lovely. Please don't go to the source for your information. Listen to the rumor mill!"

"It's because I care, Cass."

"Not that again! If you'd cared for me you wouldn't have abandoned me the moment I said I needed more. If you cared, you wouldn't sabotage my career!"

"We're not dealing in print ads and numbers here, Cass. Nothing's that black and white."

Disgusted she tried to shut the door on him but she couldn't not when he was shoving his body into the opening. "Move."

"No." He thrust the door open, and she nearly went flying.

She noticed he didn't offer an apology, either.

"Some things are black and white, but then there are all the shades of gray," he added. "There are things we can control, and thing we can't. We can work very hard, and we can do our best, but even then, sometimes it's not enough."

She didn't want to listen. She'd heard enough of him blowing hot air around. "Do you mind shutting your door on your way out?"

He was marching on her, his strong jaw tight. "I know you're angry with me, and Cass, I know you like to believe all things are possible, but I've been forced to learn that sometimes our best isn't enough, that even good intentions mean nothing."

"I don't care anymore." Cass tried to escape into the bathroom but again he wouldn't let her shut the door on him. He followed her into the bathroom, cornering her near the sink.

"You do care. That's the problem. You care and I care and we're both going mad with wants…needs…that go nowhere." He pressed her back against the edge of the sink. "I did try to let you go, Cass. I thought if I let you go and you met someone new, met someone good, loyal, less complicated, you'd be happy. I wanted you to be happy. I wanted you to have the happiness you deserved."

He wasn't touching her yet but she felt him, felt his size and strength, felt his heat, his energy, that raw primal instinct that set him apart from other men, that made her feel beautiful. Desirable. Because when he looked at her the way he was looking at her right now, she couldn't imagine ever being with anyone else. Couldn't imagine ever wanting, needing anyone else. And when he looked at her like this, his dark eyes hot, determined, intense, she knew how much he still wanted her.

She knew how much he needed her.

She knew he might never use the words she wanted to hear, but he did feel, and he did care.

He was leaning forward, his head dipping and she knew he was going to kiss her. She knew, too, she shouldn't let him kiss her. The pressure of his mouth against hers always undid her. It wasn't just a kiss when his mouth touched hers, it was love. She loved him. She loved the feel of him, the smell of him, the warmth in his skin, the sensation of his hard body against hers.

But she didn't trust him. And she didn't understand him and she couldn't—wouldn't—be vulnerable anymore.

Balling her hands into fists, she turned her head away as his head lowered. "You can't have me this time," she whispered, his lips brushing hers and then the corner of her mouth as she refused to meet his kiss. "I have to be practical." *Strong.*

He cupped her face in the palm of his hand. His thumb stroked her cheek and she bit her lip to hide her immediate and emotional response.

He was everything to her. He was more important to her than anything else…and yet he was also driving her mad.

She felt crazy. Unbalanced. Unstable. This was wrong. And it had to stop. She had to get the tough Cass back. "Please go," she whispered.

His hand fell from her face. He took a step away, his dark gaze narrowed, studying her. And then giving his head a slight shake, he turned away. "We'll leave for the Duomo in an hour," he said, heading for the door. "I'll meet you downstairs when you're ready."

She wasn't going to think, and she wasn't going to get emotional, Cass told herself as she showered and dressed for the wedding.

But trying to keep from thinking when she was in Maximos's house, preparing to attend his sister's wedding with him was asking the impossible.

Had any good come of this visit? Had she accomplished anything coming here? Or was it just torture?

Torture, she silently answered, slipping into the knee-length black cocktail dress she'd packed. The dress seemed severe, almost grim, very fitted through the bodice and waist, slim in the skirt. Yes, the Gaultier design showed her figure to perfection, but it was a bold dress, very modern and Cass took a deep breath for courage as she fastened the back telling herself the dress was like armor. She had to be tough. Had to keep her emotions in check.

Stay focused, she added, slipping on Prada heels, heels that were very high, and black, and sexy. You've managed to survive this long. Just get through the next couple of hours and you'll be home free.

Cass checked her hair, having left it loose tonight, and picked up her small black clutch handbag from the foot of the bed. The only color she wore was the yellow and white diamond bracelet on her wrist, one of the first presents Maximos had given her.

He was waiting downstairs as promised but a phone call came from the caterer as they were heading out and Maximos took the call as the caterer seemed to be having some sort of crisis.

The phone call lasted far longer than Maximos wanted and by the time he'd sorted out the caterer's problems, they were now running late.

Maximos's driver dropped them off in front of the cathedral and as they hurried up the church's front steps a man stepped from the shadowy entrance.

Emilio.

Cass's stomach did a free fall, a long horrible dive and instinctively she stepped closer to Maximos. Maximos took her hand, put his body in front of hers as they reached the top step.

"You're back," Maximos said, standing tall, his hard features betraying no emotion.

Emilio smiled thinly. "I forgot something."

"You could have called," Maximos answered. Dressed in a black tuxedo, he looked elegant. Composed. Controlled. "I would have been happy to have it sent."

Emilio's gaze never left Maximos's face and Cass felt her insides prickle with alarm, her sixth sense warning her that trouble, real trouble was about to come.

"Maybe I didn't trust you to send her back," Emilio said, voice silky.

"Her?"

Emilio's white teeth flashed. "My fiancée."

"Ah." Maximos's hand closed more firmly around Cass's, his fingers linking her more tightly to him. "Right. You're supposed to be getting married. Padua, isn't it?"

Cass tensed. Maximos was baiting Emilio. He was looking for a fight. She suddenly wished she hadn't been so confrontational, earlier. Maximos might be feeling a need to vent…

"Maximos," she whispered, squeezing his hand, knowing he couldn't really want trouble now, not before his sister's wedding. Everyone was already gathered in the cathedral. Adriana would be arriving in the vintage wedding car any moment.

"It was clever to set the make-believe wedding in Padua, though," Maximos added, continuing his baiting, ignoring Cass's hushed protest. He wanted trouble. He was asking for it. "Considering Lorna was from Padua. That's just so you. Wanting to inflict the most pain possible."

Maximos's tone dripped contempt and Emilio seemed to shrink in size and strength as Maximos's power grew. Somehow, standing on the steps in front of the Duomo's Baroque façade, Maximos's authority permeated every stone and column of the beautiful cathedral.

"I do enjoy your suffering," Emilio answered unkindly, but less sure of himself than before.

Maximos's upper lip lifted in a snarl. "Go to hell."

"I'm on my way." Emilio turned as if to leave, but stopped midstride. "And so are you."

Maximos wasn't intimidated. "Goodbye."

Emilio pretended to think. "A thought just came to me. Isn't Lorna buried near here?" He glanced around, brow furrowed in mock concentration. "I think her funeral was held in the Duomo last spring. What was it? May? June?" He shrugged. "Anyway. I forget. But then, she wasn't my responsibility, was she?"

Lorna again, Cass thought, turning icy cold on the inside, even as she felt Maximos physically, emotionally withdraw, leaving the plaza, the Duomo's front steps. It was always about Lorna. And Emilio. And some god-awful feud.

What had happened here? What had taken three Sicilian families and pitted them against each other?

She glanced up at Maximos and the expression on his face made her recoil. Rage twisted his face, his features set in lines so violent she felt her legs buckle.

Maximos's upper lip curled, half snarl, half sneer. "I should have killed you when I had the chance."

Emilio laughed softly. "But then you'd go to prison, and your poor, noble family would suffer."

"They've already suffered." Maximos's eyes flashed fire. He was different. Changed. "You've put my family and the d'Santo family through hell for the past ten years."

"It was Lorna's decision."

"You'll always blame others, won't you?"

"I wasn't driving the car."

"But you *knew* about the problem. You knew there were flaws in the prototype. You knew it was dangerous."

"She wasn't supposed to drive it."

"No, I was supposed to drive it. Wasn't I?"

"If she hadn't gotten in the car…"

"If you hadn't left something in the car…"

"That's all heresy, isn't it?"

Maximos lunged forward, seizing Emilio by the neck. His hands wrapped around Emilio's throat, fingers pressing tight. "You should have cared about her a little more. You should have at least cared. Because we all did. We all went to hell and back with our suffering."

But Emilio couldn't answer, not with Maximos's hands wrapped so tightly around his throat and Cass grabbed at Maximos's arm, struggling to break his hold, but Maximos wouldn't let go.

"Stop it!" Cass said, pummeling Maximos's shoulder, trying to get through to Maximos, but he was like another person, beyond reason, beyond control. He was in some kind of hell and he was determined to take Emilio with him.

"Don't do this, Maximos," she begged, pulling hard on his arm, trying to get through to him. "Don't do this here. Now. Your sister's getting married in minutes, Maximos. Everyone's in the church."

But Maximos wasn't even looking at her. His dark eyes pinned Emilio as surely as his hand. Outwardly Maximos betrayed nothing, but Cass saw his fingers squeeze tighter around Emilio's throat and she felt Maximos's rage. "Please," she repeated in a desperate whisper. "Let's go. Now."

And from the corner of her eye she saw the classic black limousine pull up. "Adriana's here," Cass said. "Don't let her see you and Emilio like this."

Finally something Cass said registered and Maximos pushed Emilio back. Emilio clawed at his throat, gasping for air. "Get away," Maximos gritted. "Get away from here or I will take you apart here and now."

Cass caught Emilio's eye. His pale face was flooding with color, his expression overbright and he gave her a bitter, brittle smile to match the bitter, brittle gleam in his eye. He wasn't safe, or sane. He wasn't anything good at all.

"What about her?" Emilio asked roughly, one hand up against his bruised throat. "Aren't you going to destroy her, too?"

The hot fire that glazed Maximos's eyes faded to dull red. "And why would I?"

"You would, if you knew what she did to you," Emilio answered in a silky voice that sent shivers down Cass's back.

Maximos's expression was scornful as he took Cass's hand. "I'm not interested in your lies and games."

"This isn't a lie. It's true, all true."

"I don't care."

Emilio held his position. "You should. She was pregnant." Emilio's tone sharpened. "With *your* baby."

Cass felt Maximos's grip pinch. She heard him draw a quick breath.

"Your daughter," Emilio continued ruthlessly, relishing his role as the harbinger of bad news. "Good old Cass aborted her. She'll tell you it was a miscarriage, but check the hospital records and you'll see she ordered a D & C."

"Stop it," Cass choked even as Maximos's hand fell from her arm. She'd grown cold and still while Emilio talked, so cold and still she thought she'd been swallowed by ice but the last words, the wretched naming of the procedure was still so graphic in her mind, so full of violence that she couldn't stay quiet.

"Why?" Emilio demanded. "You wanted revenge. You came here for revenge. I just don't want you to lose sight of your goal." Then he smiled cruelly. "I'll head off now. Duty's done. No need to overstay my welcome."

And he nonchalantly walked down the cathedral's steps, leaving Cass alone with Maximos even as Adriana and her four bridesmaids stepped from the car.

Maximos looked at Cass as though he'd never seen her before.

"He twisted everything," Cass said, hearing Adriana and her bridesmaids' excited voices. This shouldn't be happening now, not minutes before the wedding, not when Maximos was about to walk his youngest sister down the aisle. "It's not how he said."

Maximos features could have been carved from granite. His voice was as hard, no warmth anywhere in his voice or eyes. "So you weren't pregnant?"

"I was—"

"Was."

"There were complications—"

"Did you have a D & C?"

Cass had gone hot and cold and she was hot again. "No. Not exactly. At least not the way Emilio says I did."

"That wasn't what I asked. I wanted to know if you had a D & C?"

Footsteps echoed on the old stone steps and the girlish voices drew near. The wedding party's exuberance only made Maximos's anger unbearable. "If you wanted to know, maybe you should have been there—"

Maximos grabbed her arm. "If you did something to the baby out of spite, or revenge—"

"If I did something to my baby?" She shoved him back, features contorting with pain and outrage. "If I did something to my baby? What kind of wretched lunatic are you? As if I'd ever do anything to my own child!"

"You don't even like children."

"My God." She choked, a strangled cough as she struggled to get air. "My God. You are disgusting. You are so…so not who I thought you were."

"I wasn't the one who aborted the baby!"

"You don't even know the facts! You weren't even around to care. Hell, I had to take a damn taxi cab to the hospital. Middle of the night and I'm bleeding and calling for a bloody taxi cab!"

"You better be telling me the truth."

"Or what?" she cried, shoving him again, oblivious to all but the pain he'd inflicted. "Tear me apart, limb from limb? Choke me? Beat me? Or worse, walk out on me again?" And she yanked so hard to free herself she bumped into one of the bridesmaids, the bridesmaids and Adriana all frozen on the steps in shock.

For a moment no one said anything and then the bridesmaids in their coral silk gowns scurried up the steps toward the Duomo's massive front door.

"Are you fighting again?" Adriana demanded, clutching her long silk and lace train in one hand.

"This isn't the time, Adriana," Maximos hissed.

"But—"

"No," he interrupted, his tone harsh, no patience or leniency left. "Go to the church. I'll meet you inside."

Adriana's porcelain complexion darkened, her white and cream bridal bouquet in the crook of her arm. "You're horrible!"

"Worse than that," he answered. "Now leave us alone."

But Adriana wouldn't budge. Tears filling her eyes. "Why do you have to fight now? Isn't it bad enough that everyone on the yacht knew you were fighting? How many fights is that today anyway? Three? Four? What's wrong with you two anyway?"

"Everything," Cass said gently, shooting Maximos a look of pure loathing. "But you're right, Adriana. This is your day. And we have fought too much. But we're done. Completely done. I promise."

Dashing tears away with the back of her hand, Adriana rushed up the stairs after her bridal party and Maximos turned back to Cass. "There's no way in hell we're done."

"Maybe you're not, but I am. I'm sick of the secrets and the lies and the pretense. There are things you haven't told me that you should have told me—"

"Just like there was a baby I never knew about!"

"You were gone. You left me."

"So you were going to keep my child a secret?"

"I don't know what I would have done if I'd carried the baby to full term. Maybe I would have told you. I don't know. I never got that far."

She took a quick breath, skin prickly, hands damp, her stomach nauseous. "The baby wasn't healthy. She—" Cass broke off, breathed in deep, trying to keep the horror and nausea at bay. "I called specialists. I met with the best neonatal doctors in Europe but…"

Her voice drifted away and she shook her head. "Why am I explaining? I don't have to explain myself to you. I owe you nothing. Just as you obviously feel you owe me nothing, because that's what you've given me. For two and a half years it's been nothing."

She turned around to descend the Duomo's steps.

"You leave now, Cass, and I'll be forced to chase you and Adriana's day will be ruined."

She didn't turn around but she did stop walking. "You don't have to chase me. You can let me go. It's what you've wanted—"

"It's not what I've wanted. It's never what I wanted and it's time you knew that." His footsteps sounded behind her. He was descending the steps, moving toward her. "Now join me in the church and we'll discuss this after the wedding. Or we can just skip my sister's wedding and have it out now."

"You wouldn't ruin her wedding."

"I *wouldn't*?" His tone dared her to prove him wrong.

Slowly Cass turned, and looked up into his hard features, features that looked more like marble than ever before. And yet beneath the cold, hard expression, she saw exhaustion in the lines etched near his mouth, and shadows in his dark eyes that hinted at unimaginable suffering.

"I don't want Adriana's day ruined," she said, looking away from him, trying not to let herself feel the intensity of the chaos inside her. Because she was scared, and overwhelmed and knew that whatever was between them, had changed. Whatever was, would never be the same.

"Then you'll stay."

"To the end of the ceremony."

"Fine."

They climbed the last few steps in silence, walking as far from each other as possible. Inside the back of the church, Maximos took his sister's arm, while the bridesmaids clustered around. Without looking at Maximos, Cass slipped into the back of the cathedral and found an empty pew at the very back.

The wedding ceremony was formal and long, and as the bishop's voice filled the cathedral, Cass's head swam. She couldn't believe Maximos would think the worst of her, couldn't believe he'd think she could do such a thing after everything they'd been through.

Cass didn't know how she managed it, standing up, and then sitting down, only to stand again, and then kneel. It was like a choreographed routine but a routine she didn't know. She was trembling on the inside, trembling so much that all she wanted was to sit again.

Maximos knew now she'd miscarried, but he didn't know, not what was important, not what he needed to understand.

Another song. Time to stand. Rising, Cass reached for the hymnal, hands shaking.

This is what you wanted, she reminded herself, flipping through the book until she found the right page. This is what you wanted when you came to Syracuse. You wanted to see him. You wanted to face the past. And you have.

The choir sang on, another verse and another, and the voices were beautiful—nearly angelic—but Cass felt nothing, her body and emotions shutting down.

It doesn't matter what he thinks, she told herself as the song ended and she was able to replace the hymnal in the back of the pew and sit again. It doesn't matter if he's angry, doesn't matter if he hates you, he's nothing to you anymore.

But all the pep talks in the world couldn't stop the blistering streaking of pain.

She wanted to tell him what really happened, needed him to understand what was wrong—

But no. If he'd been there, he would have known. If he'd cared, he would have known…

Her stomach hurt. Cass took a quick breath. If he'd been there he'd know, just like she knew, he'd realize what she'd been through, what the baby had been through. He'd realize there were some things one could never forget. Like the loss of a child. Even if the baby was just eighteen weeks old. It had still been her baby.

If he'd been there, he'd know…like she knew.

Like she couldn't forget.

Like she couldn't forgive.

Abruptly her stomach rose, a rush of nausea, and Cass clamped her hand to her mouth, holding the illness in.

At last the ceremony came to an end, and the exuberant bride and groom sailed down the aisle, exiting the church amid the pealing of the cathedral bells.

Maximos escorted his mother from the church and returned immediately for Cass. "Now we can go," he said.

"You don't have to go—"

"I do. I need the truth and so do you." He took her elbow, half-steering, half-dragging her through a side entrance so they exited away from the wedding fanfare.

Outside the Duomo on a side street, a chauffeured car waited for them. They climbed into the back of the car and headed for the palazzo. Once there, Maximos directed her to his luxury sedan, one of Italia Motors' elite designs.

"Our things are already packed," Maximos said curtly, as they climbed out of the chauffeured car onto the palazzo's driveway. "We can leave straight away."

She eyed Maximos's sedan and then him. It would be at least seven hours traveling back to Rome, and she couldn't do it, not now, not alone with him. "Let's just do this here and now," she said flatly, wearily. "Let's say what has to be said and move on."

"It's not that easy—"

"Of course it's that easy. Facts are facts. Tell me what I need to know, I'll tell you what you need to know and we can finally end this madness." She drew a breath, fighting tears. "We're like some horrid disease. We just consume each other and it's not right. I hate it, and I hate the way it makes me feel and—"

She broke off, shook her head. "And it's got to end now."

He was silent a moment. "What happened to the baby, Cass?"

"I lost her."

"Her." Maximos made a hoarse sound and he leaned against his car, one of his hands sinking deeply into his hair. "A daughter."

"Yes." She could still see the little ultrasound picture they printed out for her, the new life growing in her belly. Tears filled Cass's eyes and she shook her head, her teeth sinking deeply into her lower lip. "And I didn't do anything to hurt her. I loved her. I wanted her."

"So what happened? Why the D & C?"

"She wasn't healthy. Her body didn't come together correctly, and the doctors said—" Cass struggled to catch her breath "—her heart wasn't right. There was a hole in her heart." She battled to catch her tears before they fell but she couldn't. They were too cool and fast and they slipped from the corner of her eyes before she could stop them.

"I begged them to do something, to help her. I didn't want to lose her. I didn't. She was you and me—" Cass closed her eyes, held her breath, shook her head "—and I wanted her so much."

She turned away, unable to look at him, unable to let anyone, much less Maximos, see the depth of her sorrow, the extent of her grief. "The D & C was because I refused to let them terminate the pregnancy a few weeks earlier, and then I miscarried on my own and they couldn't stop the bleeding. I was hemorrhaging badly. The D & C was performed only because I was in danger. They did it to save my life."

Maximos said nothing and after a moment Cass was able to stop the tears. She wiped her eyes dry. "Losing her is what broke me. I couldn't sleep at night, couldn't concentrate at work. I just felt so bad. So sad. I know it sounds silly since I was only eighteen weeks pregnant, but when I lost her, I felt like I lost myself."

"Why didn't you tell me?"

She shook her head impatiently. "How can you even ask that?"

"Because you know I'd want to know—"

"Why would I know that?" Cass turned on him. "You left me. You didn't want me. Why would I think you'd want my child?"

"Because she was my child, too."

CHAPTER ELEVEN

His child, too.

Maximos's words echoed in her head and Cass sagged, all fight immediately leaving her.

He looked at her for a long moment, a sheen in his dark eyes, his dense black lashes damp. "Let's head back to Rome."

Her things had already been packed and transferred from her room to the trunk of the car. Still wearing the black cocktail dress, Cass slid into the passenger seat and buckled her seat belt. Maximos climbed behind the steering wheel, started the car and they were off, leaving Ortygia and Syracuse behind for the ferry at Messina.

"I have the ultrasound photos," she said after a moment. "If you'd like to see them—"

"Where is she buried?"

"She was too young. There was no burial."

He shot her a look of outrage and disbelief. "How could there be no burial? What did they do with her?"

Cass felt her control on her emotions slip. "I don't know." She knotted her hands in her lap to hide the fact that they were trembling. "I didn't ask. I was too upset. And I wasn't thinking clearly."

He shot her another swift glance. "You hemorrhaged?"

"Badly."

"How did they stop it?"

"After the D & C they cauterized…" Just the words made her sick, made her remember and she dragged in another deep breath, feeling the dryness of her mouth, the hammer of her heart. "I guess that's what they do in those situations."

He looked at her close yet again. "Were there other complications?"

"I don't think so."

"So you can have more children?"

She swallowed with difficulty, tasting the cotton dryness of her mouth, her throat just as parched. "I don't know. I suppose so. I never—" She took a breath and tried again, "I didn't—" Cass bit down. "I wanted our baby and I lost her, and that was more than I could deal with."

He didn't answer and Cass stared blindly out the car window at the passing scenery. She'd been so determined to keep him from knowing just how much she'd suffered, at his hands, without his love, but sitting next to Maximos enroute back to Rome, Cass felt more alone than ever before.

And sitting in the twilight darkness, Cass wondered how she could have thought things would turn out differently.

Just look at them. Opposites. So different. And yet for years the differences between them had been inconsequential. Or had she only been fooling herself, pretending to be happy, pretending to feel complete?

Maybe, just maybe, she'd always wanted more. Needed more. And maybe, secretly, she'd thought she didn't deserve more. Maybe, secretly, she hadn't felt worthy of real love. True love. Maybe she'd only believed she deserved the casual indifference shown a convenient mistress. Casual sex.

Cass exhaled in a short, strangled puff. What a terrible way to think.

A half hour passed, and then another. On the outskirts of Catania they picked up the major highway and picked up speed. Night was on them and the atmosphere within the car was nothing short of oppressive.

Cass didn't know how they managed it, neither talking even though they were but a foot or two apart in the luxury sedan. Maximos sat tall, hard, silent. She sat tall, controlled, silent.

They were like marbles statues uncovered at one of Sicily's famous ruins.

Beautiful, cold, and poised.

But God knew the effort it took to maintain such a serene façade. Maybe Maximos was indifferent to her, but she felt him keenly, intensely, more aware of him now than she'd ever been before.

Perhaps it was the new strange stillness between them. The stillness like that of the calm before the storm. The quietness before the hurricane, the stillness before the earthquake and tidal wave.

The peace precipitating disaster…

Something bad was going to happen. Something that shouldn't happen. And yet Cass was helpless to stop it, prevent it. She'd come here intentionally, put the forces of nature to work, and unleashed the fury of emotion.

They both knew it was over.

There was nowhere to take the relationship, not when they wanted such different things from the other.

And now it was going to be such a long night of being together…the two of them trapped in the small space of the car with all their volatile emotions.

Cass drew a quick breath, tried to relax. She didn't know how late the ferries crossed the strait. It'd be at least nine or ten when they arrived in Messina—probably even later. And if the ferries weren't running at that hour, what would they do? Check into a hotel?

Her stomach knotted at the very idea. She couldn't handle any more alone time with Maximos.

Cass flexed her fingers in her lap and forced herself to take a deep breath, a proper breath. Calm down. You can do this.

Of course you can do this.

Think of all the things that you've done. All that you've survived…

Closing her eyes she thought back to the year she was eight. The year her parents divorced. Her mother shattered, breaking to the point she could barely function and Cass grew up that year, making the jagged leap from childhood to the unknown. It had been terrifying. Losing innocence. And trust.

Her father couldn't be trusted. After all, he left.

Her mother couldn't be depended on. She collapsed.

Cass had grown up virtually overnight, becoming her mother's Big Girl. Mother's Little Comfort.

And her mother never stopped needing her. Her mother's need so great that Cass learned early not to think of herself.

Not to think, and not to feel. Just work. Serve others. Because she was strong, and she could.

Is that how she became the woman who'd put another's needs so completely before her own?

The woman that would let a man sleep with her, but not love her?

The woman who'd let a man—even if it were a man as powerful, and compelling as Maximos—use her at his will?

"You know what bothers me most," she said, her voice strained as she broke the heavy silence. "I deliberately never asked anything of you, never demanded anything of you. I was always careful not to be a burden, not to make trouble."

Her eyes burned, gritty. She squeezed her hand into a tight fist against her lap. "I should have made trouble," she whispered recklessly, furiously. "I should have made trouble from the beginning. It would have saved us two years of wasted time and energy."

"It wouldn't have changed anything."

His flat voice made her look at him, see him, the beautiful hard face, the intensely male angles and planes, the sensual curl of his lower lip. Even now, she could feel the attraction, the hunger, the craving for contact. For him.

"We are who and what we are," he added.

"What does that mean?"

"It means you and I will always have this chemistry between us. Nothing could have stopped it. And believe me, I tried."

"You tried to end it?"

"Many, many times."

Cass felt as if something sharp and hot lanced her heart. "So that day you finally left, it wasn't a fluke? You were ready to go."

He made a rough sound, jaw shifting as his teeth ground together. "No. I wasn't ready to go."

Her heart jolted again, another spasm of brutal feeling. "But you left."

"I had to."

"Why?" she asked, feeling again that unbelievable shaft of pain when Maximos left. When he literally climbed from her bed, dressed and walked out. It was pain unlike any pain she could remember in her adult world.

She'd felt completely, totally bereft as the door had closed behind him. The contrast between him being with her—warm, tactile, real—and him being gone was too intense. The change in energy, the change in her too profound. With him. Without him. It felt as if her very self had been split in two.

Her eyes felt scratchy, itchy, her throat thickening with tears. *"Why?"* she repeated, hearing the awful pleading in her voice. She sounded like a child, not a woman and her hurt and need ashamed her.

He swerved to the side of the road, threw the car into park and leaned on the steering wheel. A flicker of emotion darkened his eyes. "Every relationship eventually ends. Ours simply ran its course."

"No."

"Yes." He leaned on the steering wheel. "It was inevitable. You can't fight it."

But I can. I have.

It's why she'd wanted to see Maximos again. It's why she'd agreed to go with Emilio to the Guiliano villa. She'd never intended to say goodbye. She'd harbored hope—there was that word again—saying goodbye. She was still harboring hope that once Maximos saw her, he'd remember how he'd felt about her, how he used to want her.

But she'd been fighting a losing cause. Fighting for something that didn't exist.

"Cass, I watched you change before my eyes. Our relationship hurt you. It took advantage of you. I knew it. And so did you."

Her lashes fell closed and she drew in a sharp breath, heart on fire.

"You can't deny it, *bella*. After all this, we should at least be honest with each other. We should finally speak the truth."

The truth. Her heart ached, knotted. The truth was that she loved him. Loved him more than she'd loved herself. "I did change." She swallowed with difficulty, throat parched, mouth as dry as cotton. "As time went on, I needed more, and you hated that. You couldn't, wouldn't, give more." Tears filled her eyes. "You just gave less."

He looked at her, dark eyes narrowed, but he didn't speak and she was so full of pain, she couldn't stop talking, hands fisted, stomach churning sickeningly.

"The problem, Maximos, was that the less you gave, the less I asked for. I kept thinking you'd realize how great I was. How goddamn accommodating."

She laughed without humor, laughed at the pain inside her, the pain that had been there for so many years, pain since she was just eight and asked to grow up overnight. "I thought you'd appreciate my independence, value my strength. But you didn't. You just kept taking. Taking. Taking."

And still he said nothing, his hard features illuminated by the dashboard lights. He didn't care, she thought, insides on fire, the inferno of too much need, too much love lost, he'd never cared. She'd been easy, available, expendable.

Yet there'd been moments of such heat and passion, such fierce physical desire that even now, despite everything, she couldn't forget. Couldn't forgive. How could she forget him? Forgive him? He'd made her feel. He'd made her *hope*.

And then he'd taken it, her hope, and crushed it. He'd taken who she was, what she needed, and what'd she become, and killed it. "But what I still don't understand is *why*, Maximos. *Why?* Why did you just let me go? Why did you give up so easily?"

"Cass, you wanted to make me the right man, but wanting something, wishing something, doesn't make it true. I wasn't the right man for you when we met. I was never the right man."

She flexed her fingers. "Yet you let me believe you could be the right man for years."

"I admit, a mistake."

She snapped. She couldn't do this, couldn't sit here, couldn't listen to this. Cass flung her car door open, stepping out onto the side of the highway. Cars surged past, headlights blinding, car horns blaring.

He opened his car door, following her onto the side of the road. "This is dangerous, Cass."

"But everything with you is dangerous, Maximos." She tried to smile, but couldn't. Instead she stood in the dry brittle grass on the side of the road and watched the traffic whiz past. It was crazy, disorienting. The entire world seemed to be spinning. "I never had a chance, did I?"

He didn't immediately say anything, and she looked at him, seeing his face in the car headlights and her heart jumped. For a wild moment she thought—hoped—he was going to surprise her, was going to speak words she'd dreamed for weeks, months, he'd speak.

I miss you.

I need you.

I love you.

And with everything in her hoping, hoping for a miracle, hoping for change he nodded once. A rough, abrupt nod. "No." His answer was quiet, definite.

She felt like a circus monkey as she smiled at him, an agonized smile so forced it split her on the inside, taking her heart from her rib cage and tearing it in two.

"Because you weren't mine to keep," he added, looking at her so long and hard that Cass felt everything inside her sag and shrink.

"And we weren't ever meant to last," he continued just as roughly. "I certainly never thought we'd go a year, much less nearly three."

He could have knocked her over with a feather. She looked at him, not knowing whether she should laugh or throw something at him. "You didn't even give us a year?"

"I didn't expect six months."

"Are you certain it wasn't three?"

"Maybe it was just three. Maybe it was just one. Maybe it was one night. One seduction. One night of hot sex and a brief, impersonal goodbye."

And yet they went far beyond one night. They went far beyond brief, far beyond impersonal. They went where few couples go.

Hot, intense, fiery, intimate.

Maybe they didn't talk about families, maybe there was no

discussion of hopes and dreams, but when they were together, they were together, arms and legs wrapped, hip to hip, chest to breast, skin heating skin. No one knew her body or her desires like Maximos. And Cass was certain no one knew Maximos's body or desire like she did.

She knew when he needed tenderness. She knew when he needed fire.

She knew when he needed to dominate.

She knew when he needed her hands, her lips, her tongue, her mouth.

"I would have given you twenty years, not two," she said, eyes closing, heart pieces of what it used to be. She'd loved this man. She would have died for this man.

And he'd left her. And then she'd lost his child and for a while she'd wanted to die, too. Could life be any harsher? Sharper? Could life be any more unforgiving?

"It was only supposed to be sex." Maximos's dark eyes glinted at her, warning her. He was beginning to lose his temper. He hated losing his temper. But this time Cass didn't care. She'd waited for months for this, waited months for honesty.

"But it wasn't just sex, Maximos, was it?"

His jaw clamped, grew thick. His black eyebrows flattened to one threatening line. "You knew what it was, you knew what we agreed it'd be."

"Release." She said the word with a bite, her distaste as obvious as his anger. "I was just something warm in your bed. Something to help you unwind at night. Something to let you get your rocks off."

"Maldezione," he cursed in Italian. "Do not talk like that."

"Why not? I'm not your wife. I wasn't even your lover. I was just your mistress. I was merely a body. Two arms, two legs, a pair of decent breasts and oh, let me not forget, the ass and the—"

He grabbed her, swung her against him so hard it knocked the air out of her. His hand buried deep into her hair, twining long silky strands around his fingers until he held her securely, until he held her and she couldn't escape. "You know the truth. You know how it was for me. But it's not enough for you to know the truth. You must hear it. You want the words."

Tears burned in her eyes. "Yes! I want the words. I want to know what it was you felt when you put your mouth on me. I want to know what it was you wanted when you came to me, when you came in me, when you made me weep with need. I *want* to know. I *have* to know and I will ask you every minute of every day until you give me what I'm desperate to know."

"The truth? You want the truth? Oh, I wanted you. I wanted you so badly that I couldn't stay away from you, I couldn't forget you, I couldn't keep you from my mind. From my heart. From my skin. I would wake at night and want you. I would wake at dawn and need you. I would fall asleep hungry for the taste of you. Hungry for the smell of you. Because there was just you. Only you. I was completely addicted to you."

With every word he'd pulled her closer. With every word he'd lifted her face higher. With every word he'd bent his head lower.

"I wanted you, *bella*, I wanted you with me night and day. I wanted you so much that it killed me to leave you after I'd made love to you. Killed me walking out the door knowing at anytime you could have someone else, that you could choose someone else, that you could walk away from me."

His lips grazed hers, a hard brush of heated skin and her mouth quivered at the scent of him, the feel of him. She dragged in air, body trembling, legs like something built out of bread sticks, stomach a bowl of jelly. She was a mess. She was lost. Frantic.

"You didn't have to leave," she choked, wanting more, so shamed and fierce. Everything was all mixed up, emotion and passion, desire and frustration and she thought she'd never loved anyone so much as she loved him just then. "I was yours and only yours. From the beginning. From the very first night. From the very first time I saw you."

His lips covered hers, held, still, just touch, just skin. She felt herself melting, dissolving, becoming only heartbreak and need. At last, the feel of him, at last, the warmth of him, at last the taste she'd craved.

The pressure of his mouth increased, the old delicious torment, the way he had of touching her, the way he had of owning her with just a kiss. It was his mouth, it was his strength, it was his expertise.

He didn't rush anything. He didn't have to. Just one kiss from him and she'd do anything he asked of her. One kiss and she'd strip bare. One kiss and he had her forever.

"You don't think I know?" His voice was deep, guttural. "You don't think I know what I had, what I lost?"

For the first time she heard something in his voice she'd never heard before—pain. Regret. Longing.

Surprised by the rare glimpse of emotion, she tried to wrap her arms around his neck but he caught her wrists in his hand and held them up, away, suspended. "You still don't know half of it, *bella*. You have no idea of who I am. No idea of what I've done, of what I'm capable of doing."

"I don't care." She tugged at the hold he had over her. It was maddening to want so much of him and have the sensation so controlled. "I've never wanted anyone the way I want you. Haven't ever loved—"

"Not love," he interrupted fiercely, his features drawn, a dull flush spreading over his cheekbones. "We agreed—"

"What? You think you can chain the heart? Tell the soul who to want, who to crave? How is it possible to legislate love?"

"But there are laws," he answered, "there *are* ordinances. Rules."

"Maybe for marriage—"

She didn't know if he broke away or pushed her away. She nearly cried at the sudden loss of contact, aware of him, aware of how her body felt him, the press of him, the size, the strength, their knowledge of each other as profound as it was intimate.

No one had ever loved anyone the way she loved him.

No one could ever love anyone as much as she'd always love him.

"But we're not married," she said, returning to him, wrapping her arms around his waist, lifting her face to see him. "We can do what we want, we can say what we feel. We're free."

"I'm not."

A muscle pulled between her eyes and she said nothing, just held him, just held on to him for dear life. "I've never been free," he added harshly, his voice grating.

Her lips did a strange quiver. Such a wretched loss of control, she thought, trying to bite down, hide her sudden welling of emotion.

"I used you." He looked down into her eyes, his dark gaze both hiding and revealing rage.

"Every time I came to you, Cass, I used you. And lied to you. Again and again. And I would have kept coming to you, and using you, if you hadn't asked for more. If you hadn't asked for love."

She was afraid to move, afraid to breathe. Every word he said blistered her heart anew.

"Ask me now, Cass, what it was you've been wanting to know. Ask me now the questions that have kept you up at night."

And now that he was giving her the opportunity to ask, now that he'd opened the door, paved the way, she couldn't. She didn't want to know why he wouldn't—couldn't—love her back. "No."

She moved to drop her arms but he caught her hands in the small of his back and held them there. "Ask."

"No."

"You've torn your heart in shreds. You stopped sleeping. Eating. You nearly quit your job. Come on, ask what it is you were so *desperate* to know."

She felt the tears well, so hot, so salty, felt the tears inside her, all the way through her to the place where dreams are shaped and secrets kept. "You're going to break what's left of my heart, aren't you?"

"How lucky you have a little bit left to break."

She felt her brow crumple, her lips tremble and the tears were filling her eyes, so hot, so impossible to hold back. "You're cruel."

"God, yes. I'm the cruelest man you'll ever meet."

And that was all it took. The last and final cut. She had nothing more to lose, nothing more to hide, nothing more to reveal, and she could feel him, feel her hands wrapping around his ribs, feel the way his chest expanded with a breath, the heat of his skin penetrating his shirt, warming her hands. She could feel his strength, the sheer size of him, tall, big, imposing. She could feel the way he stood over her, the way he had to bend, lean down to kiss the side of her neck.

Cass closed her eyes, squeezed her hands into fists and tried to stop the sheet of desire winding tight and tighter, making her long for everything again. "Why couldn't I ask for love? What was so wrong with that?"

He dipped his head, covered her mouth with his and kissed her deeply, intently, kissed her so long that her head spun and her breath became his.

She was clinging to him, her hands making fists in his shirt, her hips pressed to his, breasts crushed to his chest.

He'd kissed her many times, kissed her with passion and hunger, arrogance and possession, but this kiss was everything altogether. It was an admission of love and loss, need and guilt, it was a kiss that told her no matter what else happened in life, she'd once been truly desired.

Truly loved.

Even if he wouldn't say the words.

Even if he never said the words.

Long minutes later Maximos lifted his head, slowly swept his thumb across her quivering lower lip and smiled the smile of a man burning in hell.

"I've been married, *bella*. The entire time we were together, I've been someone's husband." He laughed incredulously as he shook his head. "Cass, for the two and a half years we were together, I belonged to someone else."

CHAPTER TWELVE

"I WAS married when we met," he repeated, his voice harder, louder. "I was married at the time we stopped seeing each other. My wife only recently died."

Cass couldn't process it all. Questions—protests—raced through her mind. How could he have been married? How did his wife die?

"You were married?" She struggled to get the words out even as her heart screamed in denial. It was impossible. He couldn't have been married. Surely he would have told her. They'd had their secrets and silences, but fundamentally they were together, they were...

"Yes." He didn't explain and made no apology.

But she shook her head, unable to accept what he'd said, unable to believe what he meant. He was wrong. *Wrong*. He wouldn't have a wife, not when he was loving her, making love to her...

"How long were you married?" she whispered, struggling to make sense of this when everything inside her was howling in protest.

"Nearly twelve years."

Cass put a hand to her mouth, pressed against her upper lip trying to hold the cold, sick reaction in as time shifted, broke, hours, seconds, lives shattering into little bits of love and dust.

And dust.

He'd been...married.

He'd been with her and *married*?

Cass felt so much at the moment that she didn't know where to look, or what to do.

Her legs felt as though they belonged to someone else, on someone else, and she stumbled backward, taking steps that felt stiff and gangly.

Maybe this wasn't happening, maybe none of this was real. Maybe if she just closed her eyes and opened them again she'd discover it was a dream. Maybe she was in bed and dreaming, the dreams that slip from the fearful parts of the mind, the dreams of heartbreak and need...

"Did you love her?" Cass asked, not knowing what else to say, what to do. His revelation was breaking what was left of her heart.

"In the beginning. Before she was unfaithful."

"She was unfaithful?"

"Lorna—" He took a breath. "My late wife, was involved with Emilio."

"And so you got involved with me?"

"No."

"But you did. You started seeing me before she died so that does make you unfaithful."

"Yes."

Maximos's voice shot through her, hard intense, and she turned away, put a trembling hand to her chest as if she could keep her heart from breaking through.

When she came here yesterday morning she had wanted another chance with him.

She'd wanted a chance to say all that had never been said before, wanted a chance to ask for—no, *demand*—more, this time without fear because she already knew what would happen if she failed. She already knew the worst-case scenario.

She'd known the worst-case scenario would be that he'd leave her, reject her, tell her to go.

She'd thought she'd known the worst-case scenario, though she'd prepared herself for the worst that could happen.

She'd been wrong. Again.

"I wanted to divorce her, Cass, but I couldn't. There were circumstances—"

"There are always circumstances, aren't there?" Cass flashed, disgusted with him, furious with herself. "It's amazing the stories married men come up with."

"It's not like that."

"It *is* like that. You were married and you deceived me. My mother's boyfriend was married and he lied to her. Are all men like you? Lying, cheating bastards?"

"No," Maximos ground out, taking hold of her shoulders and giving her a shake. "Some men are good, and some men are perhaps trustworthy. I'm not saying I'm one of them, but this isn't as simple as just being married or divorced. There were doctors and lawyers, detectives and investigations and court cases. It was everything miserable and ugly and I don't expect you to understand, but I also can't allow you to think that I didn't care about you. I cared. Deeply."

"Deeply enough to be married for what? Twelve years? And never once say one word about this secret wife of yours even as you bedded me and whisked me away on romantic rendezvous."

"It's not that black or white."

"Of course not. You live in shades of gray."

"Because I had to."

"Screw you." Scalding tears filled her eyes and she headed for the car.

"I couldn't divorce her, Cass. She was ill. In a coma. I couldn't divorce her. Couldn't hurt her family—God knows, they'd been through enough—or my family, although they would have stood by me because they knew the truth—"

"You should have told me." She leaned against the car, her legs shaking, her insides a sickening mass of adrenaline and nerves. "You owed me the truth."

"I thought—"

"What?" She couldn't help interrupting him, her body, chest, heart were crazed with pain. She felt half mad with despair...disgust...disillusionment. "You thought I wouldn't find out? You thought expensive gifts of jewelry would buy me off? What did you think?"

"That I was going to be free."

"Free." She laughed. Then cried. "Shit. How is this possible? How is it you've been married and living a lie and letting me believe you were just busy…occupied with work…" Cass's eyes streamed and her nose ran and she wiped her wet face with the back of her hand. "Let's just go, please. I want to go home, please. Now."

Maximos climbed into the car, and started the engine and as he left the shoulder of the road, swiftly, expertly merging into the freeway traffic, she glanced at him, looked into his face, the face she'd loved, the man she'd loved, and it was like being thrown into a raging fire.

It burned.

And burned.

And burned.

It wasn't that she didn't love him anymore—God help her, she did—but everything she'd hoped, everything she'd trusted had been wrong.

She'd been wrong…about love. About him.

And it had hurt so much last time trying to get over him, trying to forget him. It had hurt worse than she'd thought, almost worse than she could bear, but if there was any good news, it was that despite the pain, she hadn't died.

She'd struggled and folded, struggled and ripped, struggled, bent, broke, but somehow she'd endured. Survived.

Acid tears stung Cass's eyes. She let her lashes close and she gently, then firmly, bit into her soft lower lip. If she'd survived Maximos once, she could do it again.

Not that she ever wanted to live that hell again.

But she'd come to realize that love was worth the extra fight. Love was worth the extra effort, the extra mile, and that's why she'd come here this weekend. One more chance.

One more prayer.

One more fight.

But it was the end of the match and she'd lost the fight and she had to be big and brave and remind herself that love was risky, and real love worth heartbreak.

Her chest ached, air bottled inside, emotion hot, the pain still so recent she hadn't forgotten the suffering, not in the least.

"You said she'd been in a coma," Cass said after several minutes of endless, horrendous silence.

"Yes."

She looked at him, eyes, heart, soul on fire. "And she died?"

"In early June."

Same time as the baby.

Cass bit ruthlessly into her bottom lip, trying not to think that perhaps the miscarriage was some god-awful punishment, a judgment by God, or karma for sleeping with a married man. "How did she die?"

"She caught an infection. The infection spread. The antibiotics didn't catch it in time."

"And you're not even sad?"

"There's sorrow."

"Sorrow." Her tone vibrated with contempt.

He shot her a long, curious look. "It's been ten years of sorrow. I lost Lorna years ago. I've lived with this horrendous emotion—this mix of grief, rage, guilt—for a decade. And maybe Lorna's body was in the hospital for ten years, but she'd been gone. There'd been no brain activity...no sign of Lorna. If it weren't for the machines keeping her breathing, she would have died the night of the accident."

"But she didn't."

"Because I insisted they keep her alive." He pressed his palms against the steering wheel. "I went against her wishes...her family's wishes...insisted the doctors do everything they could to keep her alive."

"She didn't have a living will?"

"Just a verbal 'If anything ever happens...' but that night, faced with the horror of it all, the realization—" he broke off, drew a ragged breath "—I did what I could as her husband. So the machines were turned on and it was only recently the machine was turned off."

Cass was sure there were more things she should ask, more she should want to know but she couldn't take in anything else. Couldn't absorb or process anything else. She felt too much shock and heartbreak. Too much pain.

Maximos had played her for a fool.

He'd known from the beginning that her greatest fear was falling in love with a married man and what had she done?

Fallen in love with a married man!

It was so pathetic she almost wanted to laugh. She needed to laugh. This couldn't be her life. It was awful. Impossible.

Maximos drove on, heading north to Messina, but between the time spent on the side of the road and a traffic accident that snarled the freeway, closing down every lane in both directions, they missed the last ferry out of Messina heading to the mainland.

Cass couldn't believe it. They were going to have to find a hotel in Messina to spend the night.

She couldn't even look at Maximos as they drove away from the ferry terminal. There was no way she could spend another hour in his company much less the night. "I'm not going to share a room with you," she said bitterly. "I refuse."

"Fine."

"I will never share a room with you again. I will never sleep with you or touch you—"

"Cass—"

"No! You don't understand. I hate you. I hate what you've done to us…to me. None of this had to happen. None of this should have happened. You had no business contacting me. Approaching me. Seducing me. You had no right at all."

"You're right," he quietly agreed, shifting down, coming to a four-way stop. "I didn't."

"But you did."

His head dropped fractionally and she could see his lips twist. His dense black lashes lowered, shuttering his eyes. After a moment he laughed, softly, and yet the sound was painful, harsh. "You were my downfall. I've failed many times, but you literally brought me to my knees. I spent hours in the Duomo on my knees, praying. Begging God for help, for guidance, for courage. I prayed every day for the past two and a half years that He'd give me the strength to give you up. I prayed that He'd forgive me for loving you when I didn't deserve you. I prayed for peace. For resolution. For hope. But after a while, Cass, there was no hope. There certainly was no peace."

Cass squeezed her eyes shut. His confession didn't help. His confession made her feel worse and she wanted to lash out, hurt him, hurt him the same way he'd hurt her…not just once, but over and over. He hurt her by coming to her on nights and weekends for two and a half years. He hurt her by taking her body but rejecting her heart.

She'd loved Maximos so intensely she'd never looked at him and felt anything but fire.

Never felt anything but lust, hunger, passion, desire.

God help her, but she'd wanted him just as much as he'd wanted her. She'd wanted—needed—to be taken by him, possessed by him. She used to be so desperate to see him that she would have done just about anything to be in the same room with him, anything to hear his voice, anything to have peace.

How ironic. They'd both prayed for peace. For calm. For resolution. How ironic that they'd both been denied what they needed most.

"For days after you first left, it was like being killed. Slowly." She pressed her arms and elbows to her middle. "It was like you'd buried a rusty iron nail into my chest and I couldn't get it out. With every breath it hurt. Every step it ached. Every thought made it worse."

"Odd," he said after a slight pause, "but I felt the same way."

She bit her lip hard, biting with so much force she broke the skin and tasted blood. Turning her head she stared out the car window, Messina's city lights a blur of yellow and white to her tired eyes. "I just want to be home."

"I know. I'm sorry."

"You didn't have to drive me personally," she added, nails pressed to her palms, knowing it was too late to change anything, knowing that they were already in the car, halfway en route but she couldn't contain her anger, or her despair. If only they'd never started this! If only she'd never met Maximos Guiliano.

"We needed to talk."

She made a raw, rough sound, which he ignored. Instead he picked up his phone and began calling hotels to check on room availability.

Twenty minutes later he'd parked on a quiet side street and was still making calls to hotels, still trying to get rooms for the night. As he'd feared, it was the end of the busy summer holiday season, the middle of the Festa della Madonna della Luce, and hotels were booked solid. "Maybe we should just return to Ortygia," he said grimly. "There are plenty of beds at the palazzo."

"I don't want to go back." Cass shifted wearily in her seat. "I want to go home. I want to catch the first ferry out of here in the morning."

"But the hotels in Messina are booked. We can drive back to Taormina and try our luck there—"

"Please don't make me sit in the car another hour."

"We don't have a lot of options, Cass."

"What about the small hotel near the harbor? The one near the ferry terminal?"

"It's little more than a bed-and-breakfast, and it only has one room available—which you rejected because you refuse to share."

Her resistance to sharing a room was quickly changing. "But it's close enough to the terminal, and if it means we can continue home early in the morning, it's worth it."

Maximos dialed the bed-and-breakfast a second time, let the owner know they'd take the last room and turned the car around.

It was midnight when they reached the large house, which had been converted to a small hotel. As the owner had said, the rooms were all full and the one room that happened to be available was far from desirable.

The room was small, narrow, and at the very top of the house. "It's warm," the hotel owner said apologetically.

"It's fine," Maximos answered. "It has a bed."

"And a bathroom at the end of the second floor hall."

All the other hotel guests had long gone to bed and after reaching their room on the third floor—a room that had been carved from the attic—Maximos told Cass to go use the bathroom first.

Cass climbed back down the narrow wooden staircase to the small bathroom, filled the bathtub with just a few inches of chilly water since there didn't seem to be any hot water left to splash off the day's sweat and grime. It had been a long day, she thought, as she rinsed the soap off and stepped out of the tub and began to dry off. In fact the last two days had felt like a year...a decade...a lifetime.

Wrapped in just her bath towel she quietly headed back up the stairs to their bedroom on the third floor. Maximos was sitting in the dark on the small window's ledge, legs outstretched, his shirt unbuttoned. "Trying to catch a breeze," he said.

She tugged the towel tighter. "It is pretty hot in here."

"I don't think it's going to cool down much."

"Then you should like the bath. That's actually quite cold."

"Oh?"

"There's no hot water."

"Excellent."

His dry tone made her smile. She couldn't believe she still had it in her to smile. But her desire to smile faded as she surveyed the small bed. "We're not both going to try to sleep in that, are we?"

He stood up, peeled off his shirt and dropped it on the back of the rickety wooden chair in the corner. "I'm not in the mood for the floor."

"Yes, but—"

"We used to sleep close."

"But—"

"You'll survive. It's only one night. The last night. I promise."

He promises.

She eyed his bare chest, his torso muscular, beautifully so, before turning away, not wanting to see what she couldn't have, what wasn't hers to have, not now that she knew the truth.

"Cassandra."

His deep, hard voice pierced her heart. She didn't want to hear any more, not tonight, not after the last two days where she'd felt far too much for far too long. All she wanted now was sleep. Sleep and forgetfulness. If she could only wake up and not remember…not remember him, or her, not remember the miscarriage, not remember his late wife… Maybe then she could start over, start fresh, because as it stood now she was trapped. Running on a treadmill of hurt and heartbreak.

"Good night, Maximos," she whispered, pulling the covers back and sliding her legs between the crisp sheets.

He hesitated a moment in the doorway, his broad shoulders silhouetted by the soft yellow hall light. "Good night, *carissima*."

After he was gone hot tears filled her eyes and she buried her face in the crook of her arm and fought the tears back. No wonder he'd never given her the love needed or the time she craved. He'd had a wife he was supposed to love. Another life he was supposed to live. She couldn't cry, not over a man who'd given her so little when she'd needed so much.

Cass was lying on her side, facing the wall when she heard Maximos return, quietly closing the bedroom door behind him. She listened to him cross the room in three short steps, felt the covers lift, the mattress give as he sat down and then he was stretching out next to her in the small bed, his big body immediately crowding hers.

She took a quick breath, trying to control her senses, the crazy flurry of nerves. Fear and desire, she thought, inching toward the wall, away from Maximos's body but unable to go far enough to escape his warmth, or his skin. The bed was too small. There was nowhere to move to, no place to escape.

But lying here like this, so close to him, her back fitted to his chest, her hips cradled by his, was torture.

Madness.

It brought back every emotion, every sensation, brought back the intense pleasure she'd found with him—lost in him—brought back the fierce sexual awareness Maximos had awakened in her.

Before Maximos she'd never thought she was particularly sensual, or sexual, but he changed her, brought out something in her, something primitive and carnal, something alive and demanding. He made her want everything.

His hand settled on the curve of her hip. "Forgive me, Cass." His warm breath fanned the back of her neck and her hand balled, clenching the covers.

"I can't." She pressed the duvet to her chest. "You…you… you're…" Her voice faded but the unspoken accusation, the anger, the confusion lingered in the dark between them.

"I love you."

Disgusted, she closed her eyes, tried to scoot further away. "*Please.* Have some self-respect—"

Abruptly he flipped her onto her back and he loomed large over her. "But I don't, Cass. Not anymore. Not in years."

"Well, I wouldn't, either, if I was cheating on my wife, having an affair behind her back!" Cass struggled to sit up but he wouldn't let her. Instead he leaned over, his chest brushing hers.

"I never wanted to cheat on my wife. The last thing in my mind when I married Lorna was to hurt her, betray her, in any way. Lorna and I went to university together. I'd known her for years before we married…back then I thought we were meant to be."

She heard the bitterness in his voice, the note of irony. "So what happened?"

"There was an accident."

"A car accident."

"Yes. In an Italia Motors' car. Our very first car. The proto-type, actually." He sat back, his powerful frame shadowy in the dim light. "It was unbelievable. Tragic beyond measure. And completely preventable."

"And you believe Emilio knew about the flaw?"

"Oh, he knew. But he was greedy. He didn't want to take the design back to the drawing board. He wanted the cars on the mar-ket, wanted the sales…"

This was getting even more convoluted, Cass thought. She rubbed at her forehead, uneasy, uncomfortable. "Can you turn on the light?"

He rolled away, sat up, switched on the small bedside lamp. "Better?"

It wasn't better. It was worse. She could see him now. But that's what she needed. Was to see him. Clearly. Plainly. No more secrets, no more lies.

Cass couldn't look away from his face. A beard shadowed his square jaw. Shadows haunted his eyes. "When did you find out about the problem?"

"After Lorna's accident." Maximos shook his head. "That's what's so unbelievable. My own wife had to die for me to start asking questions, digging into traffic reports, doing investiga-tions. Turns out there were other accidents—not a lot, but enough for me to realize the car had serious problems—and while not all cars on the market were death traps, the prototype was the worst. The prototype literally had a brake system designed to fail."

He looked at her, his expression haunted. "But I'm not blameless in all this. I'm far from blameless. I'm an engineer as well. I know automobiles, love automobiles but I got caught up in the business—making us successful. Profitable. But I should have been more involved with the safety checks, shouldn't have trusted the written reports Emilio gave me. Instead I should have been there—in person—during each of the safety checks. I should have been there constantly."

Cass felt a tug inside of her. "You can't be everywhere."

"But there should be priorities."

She said nothing as she drew her knees to her chest and wrapped her arms around her legs.

"I should have been home more, too," he added, his voice sounding weary, far away. "Maybe Lorna wouldn't have turned to someone else for love. Maybe she would have been happier with me."

"She had an affair?"

"With Sobato."

"Emilio Sobato?"

"The very one."

Cass closed her eyes. She should have known. "No wonder you hate Emilio."

The corner of his mouth pulled, but he wasn't smiling. "While I was traveling one year a great deal, Lorna began to see Emilio. I suppose she was lonely. I was probably gone too much. She began to spend time with Emilio and one thing led to another. Pretty soon it was very hot and heavy. They were going to run away together. Have this great life together. They just had to get my money first."

A moth flitted in through the open window, flew in an uneven arc around the lamp and then toward Cass. She batted it away. "Why did they need your money?"

"So they could both retire in South America or in the South Pacific on some island and have no worries anymore. They could just be together and love—" he swallowed, cleared his throat, and continued "—love each other."

"They wanted to live on your money."

"Yes." He sounded grimly amused, and in his eyes she saw what she'd seen before—the vast wings of a dark angel.

"But…how…were they going to get your money?"

"Get rid of me." Again that grim amusement tinged his words. There was no shock left, just a horrible, twisted acceptance of one's reality.

Was that what he meant when he'd said he'd had to learn to accept reality?

"She didn't honestly mean to kill you," Cass said, shivering, and her mouth tasted cold, silver, the bite of metallic blood.

He made a face, chuckled softly. "It *was* the most permanent way to get me out of the picture."

"You shouldn't laugh. It's not funny, Maximos."

"No, it's not. But in all fairness to Lorna, I don't think she really wanted me dead. I think Emilio pressured her, used a combination of persuasion, charm and intimidation to get her to agree to…disposing of me."

Cass drew a small breath. She'd wanted him to talk, but now that he had she realized she wanted him to stop. This scared her, the words, the truth, the things she'd never known. Maximos had always been a man of silence, stillness, a man of dark passions but to realize he'd been living a life like this, trying to live with secrets even darker, harsher than she'd ever dreamed.

"Why didn't she just divorce you?"

"Getting half my assets wasn't enough. Or that's what Emilio convinced Lorna." His upper lip curled. "I don't even know if she agreed. She was pregnant you see…"

Cass was breathing in shallowly still, unable to find her bearings, sick and even more scared, but she didn't see, or she didn't want to see…

"A little girl," Maximos added, no humor left in his voice. "I went to the doctor's with her, was there for that first incredible ultrasound." He made a rough sound. "I still have it. Why, I don't know."

"Because you loved your baby."

He shot her a tortured look. "Even though she wasn't my baby?"

She swallowed, felt her stomach rise, her mind and body protesting everything she was learning.

Everything seemed to have shifted, gone upside down, and Cass couldn't find her footing, or her equilibrium. Just an hour ago Maximos had been the bad guy, the one who'd wronged her.

He'd been married…he'd been having a two-year affair with her while keeping his real life secret, but now she was learning that the woman he'd married, he'd promised to protect and cherish, had tried to kill him.

How was this love? Why would love hurt, or maim, or destroy? Cass was trembling, all the muscles tightening, shivering with shock and cold. "How do you know the baby wasn't yours? Did you have a test—"

"No, but Emilio said—"

"And we know what a liar he is, don't we?"

Maximos ran his hands through his hair, riffling it into utter disorder. "It's been the damnedest long life, *bella*. I feel like I'm a hundred and fifty not thirtysomething."

And for the first time all night, Cass understood.

She understood his exhaustion, and his hurt, and his pain. It seemed impossible that people could change so, that people who married for love could turn so cruel, could turn to such horrendous desperate measures.

How could love go?

How could love end…?

Cass pressed one knuckled fist to her mouth. "Lorna lost the baby in the accident?"

"Lorna plunged off the cliff near the villa. She was airlifted unconscious from the wreck to the hospital in Catania. She never woke up." He made a low, strange sound, almost animal-like, and full of pain. "I shouldn't have ever let them hook her up to the ventilators. Her family was furious with me. They said it wasn't what Lorna would want…they said…and yet I did what I wanted…"

"You loved her," Cass said softly.

"I did." Maximos stared across the room. He wasn't with Cass, he was somewhere else and it was a black place. Cold. Hurtful. Awful.

"And Emilio?" Cass persisted.

"He walked away. Not with my money, but hers. Lorna's. She'd changed her will, made him the beneficiary."

And that was too much of a coincidence, she thought, skin crawling.

Maximos's hatred was understandable. No wonder Maximos had been so livid when she'd shown up with Emilio at the palazzo. No wonder his family had been so shocked...so repelled.

"I'm so sorry," she whispered, knowing the words were inadequate, knowing that nothing she said would help or change the past. And probably wouldn't change the future, either.

He shrugged and yet he was far from calm. His features were tight and fire glowed in his dark eyes, fierce emotion burning. "The least he could have done was cared a little. Spent six weeks, eight weeks grieving."

"He had another woman?"

"Immediately."

CHAPTER THIRTEEN

"YOU'RE leaving."

Maximos's rough voice stopped her cold at the door. She *was* leaving. It was nearly four-thirty in the morning and she'd been certain he was asleep. She'd always wanted Maximos to spend the night. She'd always wanted a night with him, a night spent safe in his arms, and finally she'd had that chance and now she was the one leaving.

She was the one dressing in the dark, slipping into jeans and a T-shirt and heading out.

"Why are you leaving?" he asked.

His voice was deep, raspy, sexy and she felt emotion tighten her chest. A lump fill her throat. "You know why," she said, her own voice husky. "You knew what my greatest fear was—"

"Cass, I'm free. I'm not married anymore."

"No, not now."

"Exactly. Not now."

"But what about the last two and a half years? You put me in the worst position. It was a no-win situation. I could never have you. I could never marry you…have a family with you…all I could do was spend my life in the background, waiting for you." *Waiting for love.*

"I didn't mean to do that to you. Never meant to give you so little. I was so sure things would change—"

"Change how?" Cass shouldered her small purse. "What were you going to do? Sneak into your wife's room and pull the plug?"

He didn't answer. The silence was deafening. Intense. Dark. Heavy.

Cass knew immediately she'd been impulsive. Hurtful. Emotional. "I'm sorry."

"Never mind. You've already tried me, convicted me and sentenced me to life in prison, haven't you?" Maximos's deep voice held a mocking note. He threw back the covers and dressed quickly in the dark. "We might as well both go."

"I can get home alone—"

"I'm taking you."

"I want to go home alone."

"Too bad." He stepped into his jeans, did the zipper, tugged a thin sweater over his head. "We started this together in New York. We'll end it together in Rome."

Dressed, Maximos picked up their suitcases and carried them downstairs to the car where he dropped them into the trunk. "Let's go."

They found a tiny hotel restaurant not far away that opened for breakfast at five and they took seats at the window table, ordered coffee and stared in opposite directions.

It was still dark out, with just a hint of violet gray light on the horizon and leaning back against the old black vinyl booth, Cass cradled her steaming cup and refused to let herself think.

There was a lot she needed to do. Reclaim her job. Win her accounts back. Earn everyone's trust again.

She didn't need a relationship, didn't need a partner…lover…

If she were single she'd accomplish more. If she were single she'd be free to travel and work more.

Single was good. Single was best.

Although she wouldn't have minded being a single mom…

She really wanted to be a mom. She wanted a child to cherish, a child to nurture, and love, and protect…

The meeting with the neonatal specialist flashed in her head, the time the doctor had spelled out the severity of the baby's deformities. Limbs that weren't limbs. A heart that wouldn't beat.

And yet she—so desperate and so naïve—wanted that baby anyway.

Because Maximos's baby would never be a monster to her. Maximos's baby would always be a gift. A blessing. Birth defects and all.

She blinked, and jerked as a tear fell and the plop of the tear into her coffee made her jump, jerk. Coffee sloshed up and out, over the cup's rim, scalding the back of her hand. Cass twitched again in pain, spilling coffee yet again.

"*Basta!*" Maximos jumped to his feet and removed the cup from her hand. "What are you doing?"

"It's nothing."

"The coffee was damn hot. You're burned." He pulled her up. "Go to the bathroom. Get your hand under cold water immediately."

Cass attempted to dry her hand on the side of her jeans. "That's silly. I'm fine."

"Do it now."

"It's *fine*."

He hauled her against him and carried her into the small restaurant restroom. At the sink he stood her on her feet and impatiently turned on the cold water faucet and shoved her hand beneath the cold water stream.

Their eyes met in the mirror above the sink. Her face looked strange, tight, her eyes gold, her skin stark and white. Maximos wasn't as pale, he was also ashen. Gray with exhaustion while she looked shell-shocked.

Maximos continued to forcibly hold her hand beneath the cold water, his gaze locked with hers. "What are you doing, Cass?"

"I don't know what you mean."

"Bullshit. You're shutting me out. Making this impossible."

"It's always been impossible! I just didn't know it before."

"Cass—"

"Would you have kept the baby?" she blurted, interrupting him. "Lorna's baby. Even if the baby wasn't yours."

He didn't look away. His dark gaze, so intense, held hers. "If Lorna had stayed, and the baby lived, yes. Of course."

"Our baby wasn't healthy." Cass's voice dropped. "She was a mess. But she was amazing, and I know what the doctors said, and I know it might have been impossible, but I wanted her anyway."

"And I said you didn't like children."

"You didn't know me." Cass couldn't look away from Maximos's hard, beautiful features. He was suffering. But then, so was she. "And you never knew how much I needed you. How much I needed you there at the hospital with me, how much I needed someone to care enough to be with me." Her throat threatened to seal closed. "When I needed you most, where were you?"

He simply looked at her, and he said nothing because they knew the answer. He wasn't with her because he was needed elsewhere. He was needed with his wife.

Cass sagged against the sink. "You would have let me spend forever in no-man's-land."

"I didn't want to lose you. I couldn't bear to lose you. You were the one thing, the one person, that gave me hope."

Her eyes felt hot and gritty. "Hope?"

"I hated Emilio so much all I could think about was revenge. Getting even. Making his life the nightmare he'd made mine. But then I met you, and for the first time in eight years, I felt something…good."

Starbursts of pain filled her, hot, sharp, fierce. She wanted to protest but she could only look at his face in the mirror, and his expression was hard, haunted, bleak.

Abruptly Maximos reached forward to the faucet and turned the cold water off. "I'd forgotten gentleness existed. Didn't even know I could feel tenderness. But when I held you, when I looked at you…all I could think of was hope. Hope," he repeated quietly. "It's what children feel but it's what you gave me."

Hope.

It's what he'd once given her, too.

For a moment they stood in silence, Maximos behind her, his big hard body pressed against her thighs, her hips, her back. She could feel his thighs on hers, his chest on her spine and it was ludicrous, the two of them, together like this.

"I don't know that I'll ever forget you," she said, growing aware of the cold sink biting her hipbones, "but I know I can't continue this, the way it's been…"

"So we try something different."

"Like what? Living together? Getting married?"

"Yes."

"I was *joking*."

"I'm not."

Glancing up she tried to smile at him in the mirror and yet

her mouth barely moved and her eyes just looked sad, far too sad for her pale face. Funny, she thought, for once she looked just as bad on the outside as she felt on the inside. No amount of makeup in the world would cover the pain clawing at her right now.

"So what do you suggest? Walk away? Give up?"

She had to turn away from the mirror, couldn't bear to see herself—him—not like that anymore. "Yes."

Cass headed for the bathroom door, swung it open and let it close behind her.

It was time for a clean break. A fresh start. She'd leave Rome, look for work elsewhere. London maybe. Or New York. Perhaps Tokyo. She'd put as much distance between her and Maximos as possible and she'd work hard, very hard, burying herself in what she did best and eventually this horrible pain would pass. Eventually this heartbreak would be just a distant memory. Odd. Bittersweet. But not the destructive thing it was now.

Back in the car, they lined up for the ferry and then made the crossing. On the other side Maximos got them back on the highway as quickly as possible. Since it was Sunday traffic was light and they made good time on their way to Rome.

Hours later as they exited the freeway for Cass's neighborhood, Maximos's hand settled on her leg, his broad palm resting high on her thigh and she felt her heart lurch inside her chest, a painful squeeze that seized her throat, cutting off air.

His hand was so strong, so warm.

When he touched her she used to think anything was possible. When he touched her she knew she'd do anything for him. Anything at all.

Even now his touch was joy and heartache, need and devastation. From the beginning he'd made her feel, and made her believe. Possibilities. Opportunities. Love.

Love.

But there was no such thing as real love. Perfect love. There was only the broken love of imperfect people, and God, were they imperfect. Maximos with his secrets. She with hers.

Two mortals stumbling on earth with unbearable wants and needs, two fragile human beings with nothing but mortal hopes and dreams.

She felt a tear seep from beneath her tightly closed lid. Please don't let him see it. Please don't let him—

His fingers closed more firmly around her thigh. "Don't cry."

"I'm not."

She felt the tip of his finger swipe across her cheek, wiping the tear. "What's this?" he demanded, voice husky, his beautiful voice just adding more insult to injury. She'd always loved his voice, just as she'd always loved him. So not fair. Not fair at all.

"Nothing." She was tired. She could barely think straight. "I just wish—" She didn't complete the thought.

He looked at her. "What do you wish?"

"That there was just one time…one day…where you fought for me. Really fought for me. One time where we may have stood a chance to be free. To be together."

"I did try."

"No. You left. And even after Lorna died, you didn't call me, or contact me—"

"There are reasons—"

"What? Business? Adriana's wedding?"

"A court case." Maximos sighed. "Late this spring Lorna's parents petitioned the courts to have her ventilator turned off. They'd had enough. They felt Lorna and the family had suffered enough and they wanted Lorna to rest in peace.

"The d'Santos had put together an excellent case," he added. "They spent nearly two years gathering research. They'd pulled documents and medical data from all over the world. Their case stated that according to all medical evidence, Lorna would never waken. And even if she defied all odds, she'd never function. She'd suffered tremendous trauma in the accident—was deprived of oxygen far too long. I had no business insisting Lorna be kept alive."

The corner of his mouth pulled, but he wasn't smiling. "Finally I had a chance to right a wrong. The d'Santos came to me, asked me to testify—said I had to testify—but if I did, the courts would probably grant the d'Santos request."

"So you testified?" Cass asked.

"I was summoned to court. But before I had the chance to testify, Sobato appeared. He'd come to the proceedings with an agenda of his own. He went to the judge claiming I had an ulterior motive for wanting to turn off Lorna's life support. The judge asked me if I had a conflict of interest. And I did." Maximos looked at Cass, met her gaze. "I had you."

Cass didn't know what to say. She waited for him to tell the rest.

"I told the d'Santos I couldn't testify. I told them that I'd hurt their case, but by me—Lorna's husband—not testifying in favor of removing her from life support, the d'Santos lost their case."

"When was that?" she asked.

"February."

"The same month you left me."

"I was devastated." His voice was deep, raw. "We'd made plans to go to Paris. You went ahead and I was to follow but the court case imploded. It all fell apart and that weekend you did, too. You were so beautiful that last evening, and so vulnerable, and when you told me you needed more, I understood." His voice broke. "I needed more, too."

Cass could hardly swallow. "And then in June Lorna died and yet you didn't contact me, or call…"

"It's been three months, yes." His expression was grim. "But there was the funeral, and an issue of respect, as well as sorting through endless legal issues. If you recall, Lorna had changed her will, leaving her estate to Emilio, but there was no way her family or I would let Emilio inherit anything. So there were more legal battles, more petitioning, more testifying. It was incredibly complicated—financially, emotionally, spiritually." Maximos laughed hoarsely. "I'd been in hell for ten years, Cass, and suddenly I was free. And I was so relieved. And I still wanted you…could think of nothing but you. Cass, I didn't grieve when they removed the life support. I was glad. *Glad*. And that just added to my guilt. In my life, Cass, I swear I've done more wrong than right."

He pulled over in front of her apartment building. Cass had the top penthouse suite—a one-year anniversary gift from Maximos—and she thought she was home. She'd come to the end of the journey.

Cass turned toward Maximos. "Did you ever intend to find me?"

"Yes."

"You say that—"

"Cass, I can't live without you."

But that wasn't true. He'd done just fine without her. She was the one who hadn't been able to function without him and her dependency shocked her. Horrified her. She didn't want to be dependent on anyone. Didn't want to be so vulnerable. Didn't want to ever be hurt that badly again.

She climbed from the car and Maximos popped the trunk to retrieve her suitcase. Standing in front of her building with the warm golden autumn sun painting everything red and yellow, Cass told herself to be tough. She wasn't a china doll or glass sculpture. She wouldn't break just because she'd taken a beating.

Say the goodbye, she told herself, and just get this chapter in your life over with. She reached for her bag but Maximos didn't hand it over.

"I won't let you do this," he said, setting the suitcase down again. The man was strong, and beautiful, and she'd never not love him but loving someone and making a future with him were two different things.

"You don't have a choice." She tried hard to keep her voice calm, neutral, not wanting to get emotional now. She was tired, not having slept well last night, nor the night before. Maximos had a way of turning her world upside down. But she was ready for her world to be right side up again.

No more tears.

No more broken hearts.

No more unfulfilled dreams.

She was finally getting out of his life and back into hers again.

"If I didn't say the right words," Maximos's voice was deep, "then let me try them again. Because, Cass, I need you."

She swallowed, looked away and gave her head a slight shake. "No."

"And I want you."

She bit down ruthlessly on her lower lip.

"And love you, because I do."

"Maximos—"

"I've loved you all along. All these years. I've loved you more than you know, but I felt guilty because of Lorna, wrong to want someone the way I wanted you when she was in the hospital, not dead, but not alive."

She couldn't bear to hear him expose so much, hated him to become so vulnerable for her.

"I want another chance," he said, voice pitched low and urgent.

But Maximos thought he might as well be talking to a brick wall. His words seemed to fall on deaf ears and even though he touched her, she wouldn't look at him, or meet his eyes. "Cass."

And still she said nothing.

He balled his hand, frustrated. "I refuse to accept it's over, that we can't try—"

"We can't," she ruthlessly cut him off, stepping away, putting distance between them.

It was all Maximos could do to keep himself from violently pulling her back into his arms. "You love me," he said roughly. "I know you do."

"It doesn't matter anymore. Goodbye, Maximos." And grabbing her suitcase she set off for the apartment building door and let herself in without once looking back.

Cass had barely made it inside her apartment when the door came crashing open again.

Maximos stood in the doorway, hands clenched at his sides, chest rising and falling. *"No."*

Cass put a hand up, as if protecting herself.

"No," he repeated. "I'm not just going to go away. I'm not going to let it end like this. Because it's not over. There's no way in hell it's over."

"You're wrong—"

"You're wrong. Because I know you, and I know you hate that this between us is so damn intense." He reached for her, pulled her toward him.

Cass clamped her jaw tight, tried to look away but he clasped her jaw in his hand and wrenched her head back, forcing her to meet his gaze.

"You want this to be something fun and easy, something easy to control." He was still speaking and his deep voice drug against her senses, velvet rough, threaded with danger. "But you're not going to get that with me, *bella*. You can't control me, just like you can't control what's happening between us."

Her heart raced. She felt her legs shake even though he was holding her up. "*Nothing's* happening."

He had the gall to smile. "Everything's happening," he answered, reaching up to slide his hands into her long hair, his fingers twining the strands snugly, creating tension between them. "Everything's happening," he repeated, "and this time we're going to deal with it, not run away."

"You ran away, not me," she said, pounding on his chest.

"So where were you going at four this morning?" He caught her fist in his hand, to stop the attack.

"This isn't about hurt feelings, Maximos, it's about lies. Deceit. Trust."

"That's what you keep saying, but you're wrong. You're angry because I hurt you. But people make mistakes and I've apologized but that's not good enough for you. You want to punish me now—"

"Get *out*!"

"I'm not going anywhere."

"I want you gone."

"Why? So you can wallow in your misery?"

"You're the one making me miserable. You're the one—"

He grabbed her, hand encircling one of her wrists and he tugged her forward, pulling her off her feet so she lurched helplessly against him. "The problem, *carissima*, isn't that we don't care enough. The problem is we care too much. But I'll take it. I'll take whatever it is you give me—love, hate—and I'll keep it. Because I'm not letting you go."

"You're mad."

"Maybe." He pressed forward, forcing her to back up, one step at a time. With every step she took backward, he took another toward her.

"Go."

"No."

Her heel hit something solid. She couldn't move back any more. She'd reached the wall of the living room. There was no place for her to go. "I'm serious." She prayed he couldn't hear the wobble in her voice. Fear and adrenaline quickened her pulse. This was not the situation she wanted to be in. Maximos angry was no fun at all.

"So am I," he answered, firmly lifting one of her wrists and pinning it high above her head against the wall.

Cass felt a shudder of panic as his fingers closed around her other wrist and with a firm tug, pressed it high above her head next to the first, immobilizing her.

"What do you think you're doing?" she demanded, teeth gritted, body tensing in disbelief. He was trying to dominate her, control her, and she'd have none of it.

"You love me."

"No."

He laughed, low, rough, mocking. "I'll make you take that back."

"Never. Because this isn't what I love. You aren't what I love."

And he laughed again, even more grimly than before. "I'd stop talking if I were you because you'll be eating every word before long, and some of those words won't go down so easy the second time."

She flung her head back, livid, her gaze meeting his, burning. "You're so arrogant."

"I know. But you always liked that about me."

"If I'd known you were this arrogant—"

"But you did. You just called it confidence before." He shifted his weight, leaning so close she could feel the brush of his hips, the pressure of his chest.

She inhaled sharply, deeply, trying to contain her flurry of nerves. She wouldn't let him win, not this time, and not like this. They'd always been equals. Partners. Lovers.

Her deep breath was abruptly cut off by the sudden touch of his knee between her thighs. He parted her legs, boldly parted her legs, making room for himself even as he leaned against her, imprinting his body on hers.

He was hard. And warm. And strong.

She shivered. She was frightened. And turned on. She might not want to want him but her body was disloyal, her body had the worst habit of choosing him, wanting him even when her mind told her no. Even when her mind screamed stop.

Stop.

And his hands opened just enough to cover her wrists, his skin warmer, his skin doing crazy impossible things to her skin.

She couldn't do this, couldn't let him do this, not when she was still so attracted to him, not when his touch stirred her, maddened her, made her feel like half a human in search of the missing half.

He was not the missing half.

He was terrible. Horrible. He'd broken her heart too many times. She couldn't let herself feel this way, that open, that exposed again.

His head dipped, his mouth touching her temple, the sweep of her eyebrow, the hollow beneath her earlobe. Each brush of his lips made her shiver. And he knew she shivered, she knew he felt her body shuddering against his.

Bastard.

"Admit it," his deep voice rasped in her ear. "Admit you love me."

She drew a quick breath, steeled herself. "I don't."

"You do."

"Maybe once, but not anymore."

He pulled her hands higher, stretching her out against the wall as if it were a medieval torture rack. His big hard body ground mercilessly along hers, his chest crushing her breasts, his hips grinding tormentingly against her sensitive pelvis and thighs.

She wanted him.

But love? Could she let herself freely love him again?

No. Never. It was about survival, self-preservation now.

His palms slid across the insides of her wrists, sliding over the mounds of Venus to cup and cover her palms. It was the most innocent and yet seductive of touches. Something about his hand on hers, the heat, the sensitivity, the nerves. She loved how he touched her, even a touch this small. She loved what his touch did to her—the energy, the excitement, the wonder of it all.

A lump filled her throat. Cass struggled to swallow around the heaviness. "Let me go."

"No. Not until you admit what we both know."

CHAPTER FOURTEEN

HER eyes stung, salty, gritty. Admit that she loved him and have her heart broken all over again?

His lips brushed hers, and she tried to turn her head away but he wouldn't let her. "Admit it," he repeated.

She couldn't speak, couldn't respond, her body trembling from head to toe.

She felt his knee press up between her thighs and her head began to spin, tiny dots flashing before her eyes.

Breathe, she told herself, breathe. But she couldn't. She didn't know how. It was a war, a war for control. A war for survival. Him or her. Would it be him or her?

It would be her. Had to be her. No other choice, no other option, not in this case. Not ever, not between them.

"You love me."

"No."

His body bore down on hers, the pressure of his body as pleasurable as it was a torment. She might want to hate him but she couldn't forget him, the way he made her feel, the way her body responded to his. And yet she tried to block out the crazy messages her brain was telling her, those messages of want and need, those messages of hunger, desire, the craving for Maximos as strong now as it had been in the very beginning when they couldn't get enough of each other.

When Cass was certain that any sex this good was more than sex, that anything so hot, so intense, had to be love.

His hands stroked the length of her, sliding down from her

palms to her wrists, along the faint curve of her biceps to shoulder and breast. His touch made her melt inwardly, her body tensing, jerking, jumping in his hands. It was an onslaught of the senses, and even though she wanted to ignore his hands, his commanding caresses, she didn't know how to shut that much of herself down. She'd been his too long. And he wasn't angry now. He wasn't cold. And despite every effort, he was making her feel.

His mouth was at her ear, his lips moving across the line of her jaw and shivering she lifted her chin, unconsciously giving him more access to the tender skin at her neck.

"You love me."

His voice rumbled through her even as his hands stroked her breasts, his palms cupping the heavy undersides, fingers clasping, kneading the aching peaks. Her breath caught in her throat, her hips pressing forward, pressing helplessly against his hips, seeking relief. He was stirring her, turning her on, turning her into a vortex of need.

But need for what? Sex? Love? Him?

No, it couldn't be him. Had to be sex. Had to be touch, but not his touch, not him.

He stroked downward, her ribs to her hips and across her hipbones. Head spinning, she tried to turn her face away as his mouth brushed the corner of her lips.

"You love me," he repeated, his voice so deep, so husky that it seemed to break her wide open. She'd always loved his voice, loved the rich Sicilian accent, loved the pitch, the firm edge that spoke of his confidence, which was endless.

Like now.

He wasn't going to take no for an answer. He wasn't going to let her escape.

His lips touched her, covered hers, and a strange pain filled her lower back. She wanted him. Wanted him to fill her, sate her, answer this terrible emptiness inside her.

"You love me," he said against her mouth and she tried to shake her head but couldn't. His kiss was too warm, too insistent, too full of hunger and desire.

"No," she whispered, shivering, shaking.

One of his hands threaded through her hair, his thumb stroking the pulse beating rapidly, wildly, beneath her ear. "Yes."

She could hardly breathe, her lungs squeezing, chest so tight, air barely able to enter or escape. Tears stung the back of her eyes. She couldn't escape this, couldn't escape him, not now, not when she'd been so unhappy, so lonely without him, not when she still missed that baby they'd made, not when she still hoped to have another child. With him. Loved by him. Loved by her.

But he'd hurt her.

He'd kept the truest part of him secret from her.

The circles his thumb drew on her neck maddened her. The hard press of his body at her thighs made her hot, made her insides tighten convulsively. She needed so much, wanted so much and she couldn't bear to be disappointed again. Couldn't bear to give only to lose.

To love to be cast aside.

"You love me."

She closed her eyes, tried to darken her mind, blanketing all thought, all emotion but against the black of her eyelids she saw red and gold, felt the heat inside her chest spread, a ball of fire, fire of truth, fire that couldn't, wouldn't be denied.

His lips were parting hers, drinking the very air from her lungs and she felt herself sink into him, bones dissolving, defenses dropping. She couldn't stop this, couldn't stop him, couldn't stop what was started those years ago that night in Rome when he turned her world inside out, when he'd made her who she was today.

Strong. Passionate. Brave.

Brave.

She was. And goose bumps covered her arms, her entire body tingling as he kissed her deeply, making her feel what he felt.

Love.

Love.

For long moments she was lost. Gone. No boundaries between him and her. Just emotion. Sensation. Possibility.

She didn't know how long he kissed her, didn't know how much time passed but when he finally lifted his head, he kissed her lips, her nose, each of her closed eyelids. "You love me," he said, and this time his rough voice was gentle, so gentle that it brought fresh tears to her eyes and these tears couldn't be contained.

The tears spilled from beneath her lashes and still she couldn't open her eyes, couldn't face all that she felt, all that she knew to be true.

She loved him. Maybe more than was wise, maybe more than she should. She loved him. She wanted today with him. Wanted one more day. Wanted forever if such a thing were possible. God knows, forever wasn't tangible, forever was difficult to get one's head around, but forever was what her heart wanted.

Forever was what she dreamed about.

Forever was what she craved.

His thumb lightly touched the middle of her lower lip. "You love me."

A lump filled her throat. Listen to him. How patient he sounded. How wise. He knew her, knew her better than she probably knew herself. The corner of her mouth lifted.

Slowly she opened her eyes. He was looking down into her face, his dark eyes hard, intense, his gaze riveted on her face.

"I don't know what to say," she said as the silence stretched.

"You do. You're just afraid."

"Afraid of what?"

"Getting everything you've always wanted."

She stared up at him, unable to swallow.

"You're afraid of happiness," he continued. "Happiness with me."

Cass's eyes watered. Her lower lip quivered. She felt funny all over. He was right. "Please don't give up on me."

"I won't."

"And don't let me go."

"I've no intention of letting you go."

"You mean it."

"Cass, I love you. A love that can't be weighed, compared, or measured. But I don't just love you. I need you. I need your heart and your mind, your courage and your laughter. I have been so lonely for so many years, and I don't want to be lonely anymore, not when I know what I want. And that's you. Only you. Forever."

"Maximos—"

"Marry me."

"Maximos."

"Don't tell me no, Cass. It's the one thing I couldn't bear. I could wait. And I would wait. I'd wait a year for you. Five years, ten years—"

"No."

His arms hung at his side, his dark eyes shadowed, absolute heartbreak lining his features. "Don't do this."

"But I have to."

He was crying. The tears were in his eyes, clinging to his dense black lashes. He didn't even try to wipe them away. She took a step, tentatively touched his chest with one hand, and then the other. "You see, you're right. You're right about everything and I do love you, and will marry you, only I can't wait."

"What are you saying?"

"Yes, I'm saying yes." She leaned against him, his big body hard, powerful, supporting her. "I will marry you. But I won't wait. I'm done waiting. I feel like I've spent my life waiting for you."

His arms wrapped around her. He held her so close that she could feel the drumming of his heart. "You don't mind a quickie wedding?"

"Not as long as I have forever with you."

With Cass having so much on her plate at Aria Advertising— soothing the owner, wooing back accounts—Maximos offered to organize the wedding, and Cass—despite some initial misgivings—let him.

She had no idea what kind of wedding he'd plan. Her only request was that there be no long church ceremony (Adriana's endless ceremony had made a lasting impression) choosing instead a private ceremony where they'd exchanged rings and vows followed by a reception for family and friends.

Maximos agreed and the wedding date was set. New Year's Day. It was symbolic. It would be a new start, a new year.

For the wedding Cass selected a white silk-chiffon gown, the chiffon skirt straight, elegant, feminine, the sheer cap sleeves so barely there Cass's golden skin glowed through. Her shoes were a satin sling back with a glistening jewel at the toe. She pinned her hair up in a loose classic chignon and wore no veil, or jewelry other than the simple diamond earrings Maximos had given her the night before.

The private ceremony was everything Cass wanted, and when they held hands, exchanged rings and spoke their vows, Cass felt peace, real peace. As well as joy.

To love like this…

And be loved in return…

She fought tears, and succeeded, and when Maximos kissed her at the end of the ceremony she knew everything was as perfect as two imperfect people could ask for.

But the day wasn't over. In fact, the night was about to begin, and when they left the cathedral's small chapel for the palazzo's ballroom, they walked into a spectacle of black and white, a contrast of light and bright against intense, dramatic backdrops.

White orchids and wisteria artfully wrapped the palazzo's enormous chandeliers so that the ceiling seemed to drip with fragrant, delicate white blossoms.

The dinner tables crowding the palazzo's grand ballroom were draped in heavy black velvet with antique white silk table runners down the center. Tall silver vases of flawless white calla lilies filled the center of each table while votive candles cast a glow on the gleaming silver and crystal. Black lacquer chairs had been imported from Rome just for the occasion and the orchestra, as well as the waiters, were all dressed in black pants and white dinner jackets.

Cass stopped just inside the ballroom entrance, her hand clasping Maximos's sleeve. "Who did all this?"

Lines deepened next to his mouth. "I did."

"But…" She blinked at the elegant ballroom transformed into the most glamorous of settings. "How?"

"Black and white," he said, drawing her near, his hand in the small of her spine, pressing her as close as he could. "I took the idea from the first ad campaign you did for Italia Motors. It was bold, magical—like you."

Her throat thickened and her eyes stung. "Don't get me emotional."

"I'm not trying." His lips brushed her cheekbone, and then brushed the softness below. "I'm just so very grateful. There were ten impossible years, and then you happened."

She blinked, fought tears and pressed her fingertip against his mouth. "Stop talking."

"There are many people who wouldn't understand, or forgive—"

"Then those are people who've never failed, so they don't need forgiveness, and they're people who've never hurt, so they don't need compassion. But you know I've failed, Maximos. You know I've hurt. I can only give what I know I need—tenderness, love, forgiveness."

"You're the strongest person I know, Cass."

She shook her head and wrapped her arms around him. "I'm not. I'm just the most stubborn."

He laughed, and the sound was rich and warm. Then his smile died. "This wasn't easy, was it?"

"No, and I don't know why bad things happen, but I do know that good things happen, too, and you are my good thing." She bit her lip, struggled to find her voice. "You have given my life so much meaning."

"You had a very full life without me."

"But it wasn't complete," she answered, leaning closer to him, not carrying if she wrinkled her bridal gown. "It was a life. But loving you has made it great, and being loved by you has made me complete."

"Do you know how much I love you? Do you know I thank God for you every day?"

Her lips curved in a radiant smile. "I do, because I can feel it. Every moment, of every day, and it makes me believe all things are possible."

His mouth brushed her cheek. "All things are possible."

"Yes."

"You sound so sure."

"I am." Her eyes watered but the tears weren't going to fall. She was too happy, too excited, too thrilled about her wedding day. "Because even two imperfect people like us have made something perfect in our love."

Maximos's proud brow suddenly creased, eyes narrowing as his gaze searched hers. "A baby?"

"A baby," she agreed. "Our baby." She hesitated, remembering her first pregnancy and the heartbreak of that first ultrasound. "It's still early. There could be problems—"

"We'll handle them together then."

"But even if this baby isn't perfectly healthy, even if there should be a problem, she is still our perfect gift."

"You think it's a girl?"

"I don't know. But I know you'd be an incredible father for a daughter. You take such great care of the all woman in your family."

EPILOGUE

Seven and a half months later

MAKIS GUILIANO entered the world at exactly 7:00 p.m. after an impossibly long delivery screaming at the top of his lusty, and very healthy, lungs.

Weighing nearly ten pounds, Makis had huge shoulders, fierce dark eyes and a temper. But the moment his father spoke, the still wet and furious Makis turned his head, stared at his father Maximos's face, and fell silent.

"He knows your voice," Cass said as the doctor and nurses continued doing whatever it was that labor and delivery doctors and nurses do. She was exhausted. Pushing Makis Guiliano out had not been easy. But he was here, and he was undoubtedly beautiful.

"He should know me," Maximos answered grimly. "I'm his father."

Cass laughed softly. Maximos had been beside himself during the delivery. He'd wanted to do something for her when the contractions seemed to tear her apart but he held her hand—and swore—throughout.

"The little rascal nearly ripped you in two," Maximos answered, and yet he couldn't take his eyes off his new son. "How on earth did you ever get him out?"

"Determination. As well as desperation. There was no way I was going to let him stay inside." She smiled and her expression softened. "He's gorgeous, isn't he?"

"Beautiful," Maximos agreed, taking the swaddled baby from the attending nurse.

"You better watch it, Maximos," Cass said after a moment observing husband and son. "If you're not careful, he's going to have you wrapped around his little finger."

Maximos grimaced. "That's horrible." He hesitated, then lifting the baby higher in his arms, Maximos placed a very tender kiss on his newborn son's head. "As well as absolutely true."

And for the first time in twenty-two years Cass remembered what it was to feel innocent, and safe. Loved, and protected, and it was good. Very, very good.

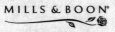

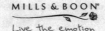

On sale 2nd September 2005

*Available at most branches of WHSmith, Tesco, ASDA, Martins,
Borders, Eason, Sainsbury's and all good paperback bookshops.*

FREE

4 BOOKS AND A SURPRISE GIFT!

We would like to take this opportunity to thank you for reading this Mills & Boon® book by offering you the chance to take FOUR more specially selected titles from the Modern Romance™ series absolutely FREE! We're also making this offer to introduce you to the benefits of the Reader Service™—

> ★ **FREE home delivery**
> ★ **FREE gifts and competitions**
> ★ **FREE monthly Newsletter**
> ★ **Books available before they're in the shops**
> ★ **Exclusive Reader Service offers**

Accepting these FREE books and gift places you under no obligation to buy; you may cancel at any time, even after receiving your free shipment. Simply complete your details below and return the entire page to the address below. You don't even need a stamp!

YES! Please send me 4 free Modern Romance books and a surprise gift. I understand that unless you hear from me, I will receive 6 superb new titles every month for just £2.75 each, postage and packing free. I am under no obligation to purchase any books and may cancel my subscription at any time. The free books and gift will be mine to keep in any case.

P5ZEE

Ms/Mrs/Miss/Mr...Initials ....
BLOCK CAPITALS PLEASE

Surname ....

Address ....

....

....Postcode ....

Send this whole page to:
The Reader Service, FREEPOST CN81, Croydon, CR9 3WZ